ASSASSINS ARE OUR GREATEST ASSETS

A NOVEL GUIDE TO TERMINATING EMPLOYEES

A NOVEL BY SHESH

Assassins are our Greatest Assets
(*A Novel Guide to Terminating Employees*)
SHESH (Venkatraman Sheshashayee)

© SHESH (Venkatraman Sheshashayee)

Published in 2025

© Published by

Qurate Books Pvt. Ltd.
Goa 403523, India
www.quratebooks.com
Tel: 1800-210-6527, Email: info@quratebooks.com

All rights reserved
No part of this publication may be reproduced, stored in a retrieval
system, or transmitted in any form or by any means, electronic,
mechanical, photocopying, recording or otherwise, without the
prior permission of the author.

ISBN: 978-93-58984-10-1

ABOUT THE AUTHOR

Shesh, or Venkatraman Sheshashayee, is a semi-retired CEO who divides his time between the real world of executing strategy and the fictional world of executing targets.

Armed with degrees in Marine Engineering and Management, he first sailed across half the known world and then ran companies across most of the other half. In a career spanning nearly four decades, he built some companies from scratch, transformed others, and turned around a few. Currently, Shesh mentors a clutch of start-ups and many aspiring professionals.

After the success of his debut novel, *Sixty Is the New Assassin*, he returns — older, bolder, and even less apologetic — with *Assassins Are Our Greatest Assets*, the second book in the *Corporate Assassin Series*.

Shesh is married to Singapore's best home baker, Radhika (www.SinsationsByRadhika.com). They have two children who make them proud.

When he isn't writing about corporate skulduggery and moral ambiguity, Shesh runs, plays tennis and reads. Though never at the same time.

This book is dedicated to Radhika,
Who is my be all.
And end all.

PREFACE

Hello again.

If this is our first meeting, welcome. If we have met before, brace yourself for another amazing ride.

You're holding the second instalment of the widely-acclaimed (mostly by my wife and by my mother) *Corporate Assassin* Series. Before we proceed, a few clarifications are in order.

First: This book is fully sustainable. No flora or fauna were harmed in its writing, editing, or occasional deleting. In fact, reading it reportedly reduces atmospheric carbon dioxide by 22.3%. (You're welcome, planet Earth.)

Second: Everything you're about to read is fiction. Please don't call your lawyer, or mine.

Third: All characters are purely imaginary. Any resemblance to people you know is either a coincidence, your imagination, or a sign you should change your social circle.

Next, some gratitude before we get to the good bits.

To you, dear reader — thank you for being here. Without

you, my life would be an aching void and my sales figures even worse.

To Qurate Books, for taking a chance on me and my morally questionable protagonist.

To my family and friends, for the feedback, encouragement, and occasional reality checks.

And finally, to everyone who read and reviewed *Sixty Is The New Assassin* — you gave me the courage (or the delusion) to write this one.

Thank you, truly.

Finally, a request. No, a demand. Perhaps even a threat.

Do not walk away without posting a review. A good one. A review that extols and praises and lauds. If you do, I will know. More importantly for you, Ishmael will know. And that is not a good thing.

Now, sharpen your wit, steady your nerves, and turn the page.

Happy reading – and remember – not all assassins carry knives. Briefcases can be as lethal.

PS: The title of this book is a twist on the phrase "People are our greatest assets". This phrase is used by most CEOs in public statements and is usually said just before they fire half of their workforce.

PROLOGUE – A MAID'S LAMENT

I am so thirsty.

I haven't had water for more than two days.

"You don't deserve any water, you pig!" Madam had screamed.

My mouth is parched. My eyes are burning.

I am huddled here, in the dark.

I am in so much pain.

"Take that, you bitch," young Master had shouted when he kicked me in my stomach.

My abdomen is purplish-black and swollen.

My leg is broken, I think.

I am locked in a closet. I can't stand. I can't move.

I am so hungry.

"No food for you, you useless wretch," Madam had stated coldly, with finality.

What did I do wrong?

I get up every morning at 4:30 am. I sweep and swab the floors. I cook the food. I wash the bathrooms. I wash the clothes. I iron them. Everything they ask, I do, without comment or complaint. I am allowed to go to sleep only at 11:00 pm.

But they hit me and kick me and punish me.

Every day.

I miss my daughters, Sunarti and Shamini. Such darlings. I hope they are fine. I hope my mother is taking care of them properly. Shamini needed to go to the dentist. I sent the money. Has she gone yet? Sunarti must have finished her exams. Did she do well?

I haven't seen them for two years.

When will I see them again?

Will I ever see them again?

Oh, the pain.

I don't even have the tears to cry.

Two days ago, Lai, the neighbour's helper, saw me when I was sweeping the corridor outside the apartment. She took a step back in shock at my appearance.

"What happened?" she asked, in a horrified whisper. I could tell her a few things before I had to rush back inside. I hoped that she would tell someone about my condition, but it seems that she has not. I don't think I can expect any help.

I can't bear the cramps anymore. They squeeze me like a giant pair of tongs, ripping me inside.

I think I am dying.

But I can't die. I can't without seeing my darling angels.

Dear God, please don't let me die.

CHAPTER 1

JAMES HONG.
I stared at the name in my notebook.

My next assignment.

The bastard who set into motion the deaths of Greg Closier and Lee Sun Wah.

The weasel who destroyed my daughter-in-law's reputation and almost broke up her marriage.

The lawyer.

Now, the last sin was enough for James to get onto my list. I am not what you would call a 'lawyer-friendly' person. Many years ago, I read Shakespeare's definition of lawyers - 'airy succeeders of intestate joys, poor breathing orators of miseries!' and found myself nodding in sync with the Bard.

But it was for the first two that he would pay the price.

What?

Oh. Oh, sorry, you really have no idea what I am talking about. You haven't read my first book, '*Sixty Is The New Assassin*'.

Okay. Your loss.

Let me start again.
My name is Ishmael Dollah.
I am sixty years old.
I used to be a CEO.
I am now an assassin.
And the next target on my list was James Hong.

CHAPTER 2

Well, when I say I am an assassin, I am indulging in a bit of title inflation.

You know what title inflation is, right? When garbage collectors are called sanitation engineers and bus drivers are called transport captains. Or when low level functionaries in banks (who don't know their ass from their elbow) are called director and vice president and general manager.

I am more what you would call a novice assassin.

I have just entered the trade.

I had completed only two assignments so far.

(However, the first target was already in the process of dying when I assassinated him. So, let's call it one and a half assignments?)

(Also, this first target was a sort of mistake. I jumped to a conclusion based on incorrect information. I am a very judgemental person. I sometimes make wrong judgements.)

(Of course, in the larger scheme of things, Greg Closier deserved to die. The fact that he was assassinated twice clearly proves his culpability.)

I have much to learn and a long way to go.

This is obvious from my actions in my first two assignments.

I did not have sufficient information. I used makeshift tools. Luck played a huge role.

For the next assignment, I will be better prepared and equipped.

I promised myself that I would do better.

Now, let me tell you about James Hong.

James was a lawyer with the firm Nestor & Ross. This is the same firm in which my daughter-in-law, Marianna, was a partner.

A few weeks ago, I met James at a Nestor & Ross party. During this party, we met, and he told me, a complete stranger, that Marianna was having an affair with Greg Closier, her boss.

This led to a series of events that left Greg dead. As an unfortunate consequence, another gentleman, Lee Sun Wah, who believed he witnessed Greg's passing, also died.

These untimely departures would have been fitting if James was correct. He was not.

Marianna and Greg were not having an affair. They were working together to set up a new law firm. James saw them leave office together a few times and reached the wrong conclusion.

That was forgivable.

But telling me, and evidently, many others, about his unfounded suspicions was not.

So, James had to go.

That is why I was staring at the notebook.

This is how my planning process usually commenced.

Without having a clue.

Staring at the notebook gave me the feeling that I was doing something, making progress.

I did this often when I was a CEO. When faced with a problem, I would open my 'to-do' notebook and uncap my fountain pen. After an uncomfortable amount of time, during which pen did not meet paper, I would go downstairs for a cigarette. That is when the plan would start coalescing and crystalizing.

I was just about reaching the point when I would rise and leave the study to head for the balcony for my cigarette, when,

"Ishmael!" called Nysa.

"Yes, dear," I said, automatically, "coming!"

My wife and I have been married for more than three and a half decades; so most of my reactions are automatic and geared towards earning brownie points.

I left the study and vended my way to the living room from where Nysa had called.

I found Nysa on her sofa, legs folded under her, laptop on her lap, scanning the screen earnestly.

She looked up when I entered and kept the laptop on the arm of the sofa beside her.

"Sweetheart," she said, "Marianna and Shahed are planning on coming over tonight for dinner. I hope you have no other plans?"

I looked at my watch. Today was Wednesday. The Club had social tennis at 5:00 pm but I could take a rain check. I checked my calendar on my phone. No meetings, no calls.

"That'd be wonderful," I smiled at Nysa. "Will they be coming over at the usual time?"

"Yes," said Nysa, "around 7:00 pm. Tomorrow is a working day for both of them, and I suspect they'll want to leave by around 9:30 or so."

I sat down next to her.

"How are they doing?" I asked.

Nysa reached out and took my hand.

"I think they will get through this," she said, "they love each other every much."

It was less than a week since Shahed and Marianna almost broke up.

Shahed had heard, like me, that Marianna was having an affair with Greg Closier. Feeling hurt and betrayed, he had told Mariana that he was leaving her.

Marianna had confided in Nysa and me. She told us how she, Greg and two others were planning to break away from Nestor & Ross and set up a new law firm. In the process, they had agreed to meet at a boutique hotel in Joo Chiat a couple of times a week, to thrash out the planning and structuring of the ownership, business case, investments, etc. Unfortunately for Marianna, this hotel belonged to the category of 'short stay' hotels where people could hire rooms for an hour, or two, or six, mainly to have sex with other people with whom they were not supposed to have sex. This led Shahed to believe that the gossip he had heard about Marianna and Greg was actually fact.

To be fair, I had believed the exact same thing.

Marianna, on her part, was deliberately keeping the new firm a secret so that she could surprise Shahed and present him with her new 'name partner' business card at a dinner she had planned for him. This added fog to the smoke, and both Shahed and I cried 'fire!'.

Once we knew the truth, Nysa took matters in hand. She spoke to Shahed. Then she got Marianna and Shahed together and had them speak to one another.

I was there. It happened in our living room four days ago.

"What a fool I have been," Shahed had almost whispered, "to have believed that you would do this, Marianna."

Marianna's face was stony. But that did not mask her deep hurt. She did not say anything.

Shahed had looked into her eyes. I don't think Nysa, or I existed for either of them at that moment.

"You have the right to be angry with me. You have the right to hate me," he had said, "and I deserve it. I know that no apology will come close to righting this wrong. But I apologise regardless. I am sorry, sorrier than I can express, and beg for your forgiveness."

Marianna's eyes had filled with tears, which then overflowed and trickled down her face.

"I should have trusted you," Shahed had continued, "if nothing else, I should have spoken to you about everything I had been told, and listened to what you had to say…"

A sob had broken from Marianna's throat. It was a sound that tugged at you. A sound of desolation and hurt and pain.

Shahed's eyes teared. He leaned forward.

"What can I do," he had said, his voice breaking, "to undo what I have done?"

Marianna had risen from where she was sitting and reached out her arms to Shahed. He stumbled up and moved towards her.

Nysa and I thought it was time to watch the next episode of 'The Crown' in our bedroom.

When we came back to the living room an hour or so

later, it was empty.

Much later, we received texts from both Marianna and Shahed apologising for their unceremonious departure. We forgave them for their rudeness.

This was the first time we were seeing them after that night.

I knew that it was not easy repairing a relationship that had gone through the strain that Marianna's and Shahed's had gone through.

It was going to take trust and forgiveness.

It was going to take the willpower not to not bring it up when angry.

It was going to take time.

I squeezed Nysa's hand.

"They are lucky to have you on their side," I said, gratefully.

She squeezed back and smiled.

We sat together for a few moments. Then I arose and walked to the balcony.

Time to plan.

INTERLUDE 1

As Ishmael Dollah stood in his balcony and looked out at the panoramic view of Singapore,

In a poky cabin in the CID headquarters in New Bridge Road, Inspector Julia Binti Shafiq shifted uneasily in the chair she was sitting on.

She had three problems.

The first was that her new pair of uniform pants was tighter than any pair of pants had the right to be. The synthetic fibre was creating new and interesting creases on various parts of her lower body. It was also sticky. Yes, they had taken measurements about 6 months ago, but she was quite, no, mostly, no, sort of sure that those measurements were still valid. Her refusal to ascend any kind of weighing scale, however, prevented a fact check.

The second was that the chair she was sitting on was well past its prime. The seat, presumably faux leather, was cracking and peeling, much like her skin on her last trip to Phuket. It was also probably stained with unidentifiable fluids, but since it was black, nothing showed. She could sense the stains from the delicate aroma that rose from the seat every time she shifted. It was also unstable, and jerked drunkenly every so often, causing her to sit gingerly and trying to avoid unnecessary movements.

The third had nothing to do with her personal comfort.

The third problem lay in front of her in the form of two files. One was quite thick, about three quarters of an inch. The other was elegant in its slimness. Both were the standard pale blue files that the CID purchased in thousands.

The first file contained everything there was about the murder of a lawyer.

The second file contained very little about the death of a retired banker.

Only two coincidences connected the two deaths. The first was that both the deceased belonged to the same club. The second was that both of them died within 4 days of each other.

Julia knew that the connections were most likely specious. But.

She could smell something rotten, and it wasn't the chair.

Her instincts, honed by fifteen years of investigative work and nearly forty years as a human being, told her that the two cases were linked. How and why? She had no idea.

Julia had reviewed the files at least ten times in the past two days. Nothing had sprung out at her, like they did so easily in detective serials. The files were boring, dry and factual. They were sparing in their facts and ambiguous in the conclusions. There were no highlighted phrases, the sight of which caused a sudden epiphany.

She went over the facts again in her mind.

The first victim (yes, if Julia's instincts were right, he was a victim), a lawyer, died in the club restroom, seemingly of poisoning.

The second victim, a retired banker, died at MacRitchie Reservoir, seemingly of natural causes.

There was no evidence that the two victims knew each other, professionally or socially. They were about three decades apart in age. The banker had spent his career in personal wealth management and had never had cause to engage with a corporate law firm. They moved in very different social circles. The only overlap was the club, and the two never seemed to have encountered each other ever.

Julia took a deep breath. She collected the two files, opened a drawer in her desk and pushed them in.

I need a cigarette, she thought. Time to stop thinking for a while. Let me catch up on what's going on in the gossip circle.

She stepped out of the temporary office and began the long walk to the smoking area.

CHAPTER 3

Standing on a balcony on the 24th floor in Singapore is an amazing experience.

I could see most of our island nation.

A thousand shades of green vied for my attention. In the distance, Bukit Timah bristled with towers and antennae. In the other direction, ships and boats jostled for space and recognition in the crowded inner anchorage. Tiny vehicles of all shapes and sizes zipped up and down roads, blinking red when prevented from pursuing their goals.

The afternoon sun lit the city, striking glass sheets that cladded numerous high-rise apartments and created a kaleidoscope of reflections. The air, while warm, was pleasant, with an intermittent breeze wafting one way and then another.

I knew it was a pity polluting this idyllic eyrie with smoke. But what could I do? What started as an attempt to look cool in college had become an unshakeable addiction. Plus, it helped me think and plan.

I lit my cigarette and took a deep drag.

Neurons awoke from somnolence and started skating

along dormant pathways. Synapses collated and directed these neurons, releasing neurotransmitters that started putting together disjointed facts, opinions, and feelings.

James Hong. Lawyer. Target. Locations. Methods? Timing? Risks. Office. Apartment. Mall? Cameras. Accident. Natural causes. Family? Children?

As the cigarette grew shorter, options began taking shape. Paths started forming. Disjointed pieces found their slots and fell into place.

Strange that smoke helps one see so clearly.

I stubbed the cigarette butt out in the microscopic ashtray that was Nysa's way of expressing her disapproval of my habit.

I continued standing at the balcony for a while, a thousand-yard stare in my unseeing eyes, moving parts, arranging pieces, untangling threads.

Then I took a deep breath. Time to go to the drawing board.

Sadly, it was not to be.

"Ishmael," said Nysa, as soon as I stepped from the balcony into the living room, "Could you be a darling and run down to the FairPrice for me? I need a few things for this evening."

As I have told you before, I love Nysa more than life itself. She is the most beautiful woman in the world, and an amazing person in all respects.

Almost all respects.

I have a bunch of neuroses. And, either due to causation or correlation, I am anal. I like to plan. I need to plan. Everything has to be just so. A place for everything and everything in its place, and all that.

Nysa never plans. Her whole life is a series of spontaneous acts, last minute decisions and random throws of the dice.

This causes me tremendous discomfort. Eighty three percent of our arguments are because of this one issue.

When we travel, I ensure that I make a folder (yes, with coloured tabs) that contain every possible document that we may need. I pack at least 48 hours in advance. I write lists. I send messages and emails.

Nysa starts packing three hours before we leave for the flight. Inevitably, she will discover that her swimsuit is missing, or her travel kit is bereft of critical lotions and creams. Indubitably, she will realise that she doesn't have the right footwear for the cruise, beach, mountain or resort. Then, Nysa will press me to find, buy, borrow or steal the required item(s) while I sweat anxiously as the departure time nears, minute by excruciating minute.

As a consequence of this difference in world views, almost every holiday has begun with a fight or a cold silence. Staff at airline counters are known to ask us if we want seats in separate sections. Flight attendants smile sympathetically at Nysa and give me dirty looks and water down my wine.

She was doing this again!

"Nysa," I protested, "I have work to do…"

"Ishmael, my sweetheart," Nysa said, "I ask you for so little, please be a dear and help me. I have so much to do before the children come. Also, I am in the midst of dealing with this new author who is giving me a hard time."

Ha! Ask me for so little! So much to do! Ha!

I trudged to the study to change into my walking gear, muttering rebelliously. By the time I was ready, Nysa had texted me the list of items that she wanted, all of which could have been purchased online with a little bit of planning.

As I walked to the FairPrice store, I continued where I left off in the balcony.

First, I needed to find out everything I could about James Hong. Where he lived, who he lived with, what he did at work and outside it, which places he visited, what secrets he hid. What and where he ate, what and where he drank. What he did before work, and what after work. What occupied him on weekends. This information would allow me to identify his living routines and patterns.

Then, I would need to analyse these patterns and look within them for vulnerabilities that would leave him exposed.

Next, I had to choose the right location-time nexus to reach out to him.

Finally, I would need to choose the right approach to make his departure seamless and natural.

And, in all this, ensure that I fly under any radar screens.

"Do you have Passion card?" asked the lady at the cash register.

I looked up, slightly startled.

I had been operating on auto and realised that I had picked up all the items Nysa had asked for and had reached the cashier station while lost in my planning.

"Oh, so sorry, no Passion card," I said.

"No problem, sir," she said, smiling sweetly. "Next time, please get Passion card, lots of discount."

"Sure," I said, smiling back, "and thank you so much."

I left the store, lugging five kilos of groceries in frail plastic bags that I hoped would hold their integrity till I reached home.

In addition to planning my next steps to deal with James,

I was also grappling with a couple of questions.

The first of them was – was it too soon?

Would having two deaths in Nestor & Ross within the space of a couple of weeks raise suspicions in the wrong quarters? Would this lead to increased scrutiny? Would Greg's case be re-investigated more granularly?

Singapore was not Baltimore or New York, where murders and killings were commonplace. I doubted that Singapore had as many unnatural deaths in a year as New York had in a week.

Also, Singapore's CID had a formidable reputation. They were smart, determined and dedicated. Their closure rate was in the high 80s.

I had to give this more thought.

The second question was – what was the line separating serial killing from assassination?

In my philosophy, there are two realities.

The first reality, which is unquestioned, is that everyone dies. Some sooner than others.

The second reality, which is questioned (mostly by bleeding hearts), is that most people deserve to die. Sooner rather than later.

If you belong to the school of thought that disagrees with this statement, ask yourself honestly.

That obnoxious neighbour who plays music so loudly that your wall starts developing cracks? Even after you requested him many times to have some consideration for others?

Or that ratfink colleague who takes credit for everything you do? And quietly whispers damaging things about you behind your back?

Or that self-righteous relative who drove his daughter to

suicide because he refused to accept that she was in love with a woman? And is now in the process of destroying his son?

Have you not seriously considered the unbridled joy that their early departures would bring to so many? Have you not told yourself, at least once, "I wish…"?

Death can be a release, not just for the deceased but for all the people around them. One death can set multitudes free.

Just think about it.

However, even with my rather unorthodox views of life and death, I still believe that there is a huge difference between terminating for convenience and terminating for cause.

The first is self-serving and indulgent.

The second is beneficent and necessary.

The question I was grappling with is – where do we draw the line?

While trying to reach a decision, I realised that I had reached our condo. I got into the elevator, switched on the overhead fan, and switched off my overheated mind.

As the elevator ascended, I looked at the mirrored walls, checking if there were any smudges. Suddenly, something Nysa had said before I left popped up in my mind.

"…I am in the midst of dealing with this new author who is giving me a hard time…"

Who was this new author and why was he/she/it causing Nysa a problem? What problem? How long had this been going on?

CHAPTER 4

When I entered the living room, I made sure that I panted obviously, hoping to make Nysa feel guilty for having made me do her last-minute shopping for her.

Sadly, my subterfuge fell flat on its face. Nysa was not in the living room.

I thought that it would look ridiculous if I panted my way across the house, so I stopped.

I walked to the kitchen and placed the bags on the island, knowing that Siti would despatch their contents to their allocated places. I wanted to get back to what I was doing when I was so rudely (and unnecessarily) interrupted.

But before that, I needed to find out what was troubling Nysa. I went to her study and knocked and entered. Nysa was sitting at her desk reading something on her laptop.

"Hi, Nysa," I said. She looked up, distractedly.

"Ah, Ishmael, were you able to get everything on the list?" she asked.

"Yes, I was," I said, tersely, "what did you mean that an author is giving you a hard time?"

Nysa leaned back in her chair.

"I've been wanting to talk to you about this," she said, "Pangolin Publishers have connected me to William Randall. He's writing the second part of his 'East India' trilogy and is looking for a new lead researcher."

"Wow." I said, "that's great. Randall is an amazing author. You love his books."

"Yes, and I would love working with him," said Nysa, "but he has all these requirements and specifications which are going be really tough to deliver. And he is pushing me to reduce my fees. 'You are more than twice as expensive as my previous researcher', he says."

"Can I be of help?" I asked, "could you share the list of his requirements with me?"

"That would be great, Ishmael," said Nysa, perking up, "I'll share our e-mail exchanges so far. And the minutes of our calls. I would truly appreciate your advice."

"I am yours to command," I said, smiling, "No one other than me is allowed to give you a hard time."

"I'll collate everything and send it to you tonight, after dinner," said Nysa, rising, "I have to get to the kitchen now."

I quickly glanced at the time. Another hour and half before Marianna and Shahed arrived.

I continued onwards to the study.

I opened my laptop and started my deep dive into social media, searching for the essence of James Hong.

James was thirty-six years old. He had completed his law degree from NUS. He was an associate. (An associate, at thirty-six? What a loser!)

For the past three years, he had been with Nestor & Ross. He was awarded no promotions during his stay. Before that, he had been an associate with a local law firm – Yeo & Moon.

James loved social media. Other than his private ablutions, he posted everything. His life was an open, albeit rather monotonous, book.

He lived in an executive condo in Bishan. He rented.

He was not married. Nor did he seem to be in a relationship.

It seemed like he had no hobbies other than taking selfies and photos of food that he was about to eat and places that he was in.

Strangely, he had only about 320 connections on LinkedIn. That was pathetically low. He evidently did not know how to make friends and influence people.

A lot of this information was very reassuring.

An unattached, not-very-popular, low-level grunt is a much easier target than a high-profile, well-connected honcho.

I created a new password protected folder which I named "third strike". I liked the connotation.

I stored everything I had downloaded in the folder.

What was the time? Oh, 6:45 pm. Time to freshen up for dinner.

I changed into my jeans and a collared t-shirt. I had a two-day stubble, but did not have the energy to shave, especially after that draining visit to the FairPrice store.

I went to the pantry to check the wine cooler if there was enough stock of various beverages that were likely to be consumed that night. Then, I went to the bar console and laid out the right glasses.

Finally, I went to the balcony so that I could commune with nature and tobacco.

Just when I was finishing my cigarette, the doorbell rang.

I stubbed it out and walked over to the front door and opened it.

"Hi Dad!" said Shahed as he gave me a hug.

"Hi Ishmael," said Marianna, as she embraced me and gave me a kiss on my cheek.

Both of them seemed to be in great spirits.

I ushered them in just as Nysa came up.

More hugs and kisses all round.

In a few minutes, we were all sitting in the living room, glasses in hand.

"How come you are in town, Shahed?" I asked.

Shahed is a regional sales manager and is usually travelling through the work week.

"Oh, well, I thought I would not travel this week," he said, haltingly, looking at Marianna.

She was more forthright.

"We needed to spend some time together and get rid of some baggage we seem to have collected," she said, "we needed to talk about us and our future."

Nysa nodded.

"Relationships are fragile things," she said, "they need continuous reinforcing. Otherwise, they can wither away."

"Absolutely," said Marianna, "both of us have been spending too much time at work, and not focusing on what is most important to us. That is going to change."

I hated being a wet blanket.

"Don't count on it," I said, "both of you are ambitious professionals. Your career trajectories will place unreasonable demands on your time. You will need to live with this and find a balance in an unconducive framework."

Shahed nodded. "I get your point, Dad," he said, "and that is what Anna and I have been talking about – how we are going to find balance between what we want and what we need, between what we seek and what we have."

"Very wise," said Nysa, shooting me a glance, which I read, noted, and obeyed.

"So, how is work?" I asked, generally.

"Well, Nestor & Ross is still coming to terms with Greg's loss. Richard is spending a lot of time with all of us, individually and together, and building the morale," said Marianna, "still, it's going to take time…"

"Have they started looking for a replacement?" I asked.

"Well, Richard has hinted that it is likely to be an internal promotion," said Marianna, tentatively.

While I am completely lacking in empathy, I heard some subtext.

"And are you in the running?" I asked.

"Well, I was working closely with Greg with most of his clients," she said, not quite comfortably, "and Richard has asked me to take over Greg's portfolio, though he clearly said that this would be an interim arrangement."

I smiled. At least one good thing was coming out of Greg's passing.

"All the best, Marianna," I said, "you would make a wonderful Managing Partner!"

Marianna blushed and grasped Shahed's hand.

"Wow, that'd be amazing!" exclaimed Nysa, "come, we must celebrate this with another glass of wine."

She held out her glass to me, her indentured slave.

I refilled our glasses, and we toasted Marianna's prospects.

"What could hinder your chances?" I asked.

Marianna sipped her wine before replying. She glanced at Shahed.

"Well," she hesitated, "this Greg issue has not gone away. There are still some partners who believe that we were having a relationship…"

"And?" I asked, sensing some more subtext.

"Also, I heard that some of the partners in UK expressed their preference for an external candidate," said Marianna, "they wanted a fair comparison, it seems."

"Mm-hmm," I said, knowing that there was more, "please go on."

Marianna kept her wine glass down. She seemed to be debating whether to continue.

"It's James Hong!" Marianna burst out, "he keeps poisoning every ear he whispers into. Even if people want to forget, he refuses to allow them to do so."

"But isn't he just an associate?" I asked, casually.

"Yes, but he weasels his way into partners' rooms and their favours," said Marianna bitterly, "and for some reason, they listen to his nonsense. Why he is bent on hurting me and my reputation, I don't know."

"That's not so difficult to understand," I said, calmly, "You and he are about the same age, and you are being considered for Managing Partner whilst he remains an associate."

"Whatever his reasons, Ishmael," said Marianna, practically gritting her teeth, "he could cost me this promotion. That would be horrible – to lose out because of someone's malice. How I wish someone could make this scoundrel disappear!"

Shahed put his arm around Marianna and pulled her to him, comforting her.

Nysa was saying something, but I didn't hear her.

Marianna had just answered my second question.

James Hong was going to be terminated for cause.

CHAPTER 5

"…Ishmael," I heard faintly.

I shook my head and returned to the room. Nysa, Marianna and Shahed were looking at me strangely.

"Yes?" I asked, "what is it?"

"Where did you zone off to suddenly?" asked Nysa, "one minute we were talking and another, you are in la-la land."

"I am sorry, sweetheart," I apologised, "one thought led to another that led to another. A solution for one of my start-ups seems to have taken shape. So sorry…"

"Dad, you are too young to go senile," joked Shahed.

Marianna slapped his thigh in my defence but spoiled it by giggling.

"Can I get you all a refill?" I asked and received a chorus of affirmatives.

I walked over to the bar.

Okay, I understand that you may be a little confused about these phrases, 'termination for cause' and 'termination for convenience'.

Let me explain.

Almost all contracts in the world – employment

contracts, construction contracts, purchase contracts - have termination clauses. These clauses broadly fall into two buckets.

The first is termination for cause. This allows either party, but usually the party that is paying for a good or a service that the other party if providing, to cancel or terminate the contract in case of non-performance or wilful negligence by the other party.

The second is termination for convenience. This is a far more draconian clause. It allows the paying party to cancel the contract whenever the feel like doing so. This is the equivalent of a husband divorcing a wife saying, "talaaq, talaaq, talaaq" because she didn't birth a boy or made the chicken vindaloo too spicy.

Now, here is where you need to follow closely.

In my opinion, people are like contracts.

Each person is supposed to have a broad purpose (though I haven't been able to find one in most people I have met) and a finite tenure.

Both, contracts and people are subject to the same, or similar, clauses – but in the case of people, termination clauses are rarely invoked except in times of war, revolution, or legally sanctioned retribution.

As I said earlier in this narrative, termination can be a release, not just for the deceased but for all the people around them.

But there must be cause.

Termination for convenience, in the case of people, is just murder or serial killing.

That is wrong. It benefits only the killer. It is skewed.

Termination for cause is assassination.

Used appropriately, justifiably, it benefits society as a whole. It is justice.

Especially when the target is deliberately and maliciously hurting someone I love.

I hope everything is clear now?

Back to the bar.

I opened the can of beer for Shahed, poured the red wine and Rosé, and carried the tray to serve everyone.

"How is Jocelyn, Anna?" asked Nysa, "have you been in touch with her?"

Jocelyn was Greg Closier's widow.

"Only once, the day before yesterday," replied Marianna, "Richard had asked her into the office to sign some documents. We spoke for a few minutes. She seemed to be bearing up well. Such a strong lady."

"Poor thing," said Nysa, sadly.

I was not so sure. I believed that Jocelyn had contributed to the premature passing of her husband. I think she had complained about Greg's philandering ways to her Godmother once too often. And Madam Hwa, a senior member of Taiwan's intelligence agency, took action to forever remove Greg from Jocelyn's life. The only thing I was unsure of was whether Jocelyn had said, 'I wish he were dead', or 'Please kill him'. Either way she was culpable.

"Shall we have dinner?" I asked. "I am starving!"

"Absolutely," said Nysa, getting up, "just give me a few minutes to warm up the food,"

She left for the kitchen. Marianna followed her.

Shahed and I looked at one another.

"So?" I asked.

He took a deep breath.

"I screwed up, Dad," he said, "I suspected her without any basis or proof. It was stupid and wrong."

"I understand, Shahed," I said, kindly, "but isn't that the nature of suspicion? The lack of proof? And isn't that the nature of man? To suspect?"

"Based on what Marianna has told us, everything pointed to an unhappy situation," I continued, "if I were you, I would have reached the same conclusion."

I did not tell him that I had indeed reached the same conclusion, and furthermore, acted on it.

"Yes, but I should have trusted her," he said, "isn't that the basis of love?"

"I can't argue that sentiment," I replied, "but most men are essentially scared, insecure creatures, prepared to believe the worst of everyone but ourselves."

"I have gone through the same fears and worries with Mom, Shahed," I said, "I, too, was insecure and scared, at different stages in our marriage. This is what happens when we marry beautiful, talented women – we feel like we have bitten off more than we can chew."

Shahed smiled.

"The last few days have been good," he said, tentatively, "we have been speaking and reconnecting. I believe we are on our way to putting this behind us."

Till it rears up again in the future, I thought cynically.

"Come, let's have dinner," I said, standing up.

We went to the dining room, to join Nysa and Marianna.

That night, after the children had left, I excused myself and went to the study.

I sat, turned the chair to face the bay window, and looked out at the lights of Singapore.

So far, my career as an assassin was helped by the fact that the players were in my sphere of influence.

James Hong, however, was not.

I had no connection to him. I had no immediate way of tracking him, or luring him, or confronting him.

Also, unlike assassins in fiction, I did not have a team of world-class hackers backing me. Nor did I have access to state-of-the-art equipment which could hear conversations through lead-sheathed rooms or clone James' phone with one swipe.

I was at a serious disadvantage. The risks were clear and present. This assignment would need a lot more thought, planning and effort.

I shrugged. Been there, done that.

Fifteen years ago, I was asked to take over a nearly defunct company and turn it around. It had been a wonderful organization, being valued at close to two billion dollars at its peak. Unfortunately, mismanagement and greed had stretched its balance sheet to breaking point and left the company insolvent.

Everyone I spoke to or approached for advice cautioned me against taking this role. Especially as I was already the CEO of an established, growing company.

"It's terribly risky," they said.

"Your reputation is on the line," they said.

"You already have a great job," they said.

I heard them, considered all the pros and cons, and took the role anyway. (The only person who said, 'go for it' was Nysa)

Within three years we had turned the company around and sold it for a gazillion dollars.

In the process, I realised that it was necessary to shut down many regional offices and operations centres. It was necessary to terminate hundreds of employees. It was necessary to pivot the company to an entirely new market.

I planned what needed be done, prepared for it and then did it.

Terminating James Hong?

It was necessary.

It would be done.

INTERLUDE 2

As Ishmael Dollah sat and looked out at the shimmering lights of Singapore and planned his next assignment,

Inspector Julia Binti Shafiq paced in front of the projection screen, coming closer and closer with every pass.

The video was grainy and poorly lit.

"Rewind the last two minutes, please," she asked.

The technician hit pause and rewind.

"Is there anything particular you are looking for, madam?" he asked.

"I'll know when I see it," she replied, shortly, her entire being focused on the screen.

The video started again.

The man walked towards the corridor to the restrooms and entered it, lost from view. She could only see his back. But the timeline was right – this must be Greg Closier. Also, the figure was taller than average, and she recalled that Closier's height was a little above six feet.

A minute later, another indistinct figure walked to the corridor. Again, only the back. This person was shorter, but his walk was brisker, more determined.

I hope I am not allowing my imagination to run wild, she thought.

Two minutes passed.

And one more.

A man came out of the corridor, facing the camera. He seemed older? He walked past the camera and was lost from view.

Four minutes more.

The shorter man walked out. His complexion was darker than the previous man. He turned and went into the restaurant.

A woman came out of the restaurant. She was petite and wearing a skirt and jacket. She walked past the camera.

The clock continued counting.

Nothing for the next six minutes.

Two men exited from the restaurant and walked towards the corridor and enter it.

Twenty seconds.

Both men came running out of the corridor. They were clearly agitated; one was shouting something.

"Stop." she said.

The technician paused the video.

Was there something here? Did the short man leave the restroom before Closier fell? Or did he witness Closier's fall and not want to get involved? Or, even worse, did he have something to do with it?

And who was the other man, the older one, who came out? Did he see anything?

She turned to the technician.

"Is there anything we can do to enhance the imagery?" she asked.

"Um, we can't, madam," he replied, "but the National Security Coordination Secretariat labs surely can. They have some amazing equipment and people there."

"Umm, thanks, Chee Wee," said Julia, "can you talk to them today? I need to catch up on a couple of my other cases."

As Chee Wee walked out, Julia dropped into a chair.

What should she do about the report of the maid being abused? The problem was that it was not an official report. A neighbour had called the police hotline and informed them that his helper had reported to him that their neighbour's maid was showing signs of abuse and distress.

"Have you seen the neighbour's maid yourself, sir?" he was asked.

"Um, no, not really," he had answered.

"Have you heard anything from anyone else?"

"Um, no, I haven't."

"Would you like to submit a formal complaint?" was the next question.

"Oh, no," was the immediate answer, "they are our neighbours. I don't want to get them into trouble unnecessarily."

Neither was this her case. Yet. If it were registered, it could go to the Ministry of Manpower. If the situation was severe, it could be allocated to Julia or one of her colleagues.

She needed to do something. She could not just sit back and wait.

Let me drive down to Choa Chu Kang when I have the time and make some casual enquiries, she said to herself.

Perhaps I could ask to speak to the helper herself? Better to be safe, rather than sorry?

CHAPTER 6

Have you ever been catfishing?

I am not talking about the US version where you would sit for hours on an end in the cold and damp and hope to catch a catfish (which, by the way, is a truly ugly fish) with the sole objective of boasting about it in the bar.

I am talking about luring an entirely different victim.

In most cases, not much smarter than a catfish, but still. More human. More needy. Almost desperate to take the bait.

So far, I had only read about this practice. And each time I did, I would come away with a sneaking admiration for the catfisher, rather than any sympathy for the catfishee (is that even a word?).

Oh, okay, sorry, you have no idea what catfishing is. You are either geriatric or a Luddite. No worries, I am here to explain.

From Wikipedia:

Catfishing is a deceptive activity in which a person creates a fictional persona or fake identity on a social networking service, usually targeting a specific victim.

The practice may be used for financial gain, to compromise a victim in some way, as a way to intentionally upset a victim, or for wish fulfilment.

Basically, let's say that you are an average man and have some disposable income.

Let's say I am another man and would like to partake of your disposable income.

If I asked you to share, you would refuse. That would make me sad. And angry. And frustrated.

So, I don't ask you.

Instead, I create a persona on Facebook, where I know you spend much of your office hours.

Here, I am not a man.

I am an innocent young girl, seeking an experienced man who could guide me and teach me the ways of this wicked world.

I am pretty (but not too), young (but not too), well to do, but naïve and wide eyed. (That last part contributes to my being pretty).

I connect with you.

You are surprised but delighted. In all your thirty plus years, no woman has given you the time of the day voluntarily.

I speak breathlessly to you (metaphorically).

Your chest puffs up. You feel smarter and wiser. Almost like a demigod.

I bat my eyelashes at you (virtually).

You feel like Adonis and Apollo rolled into one, regardless of what your mirror wants you to believe.

You are firmly on the hook.

At this point, there are many roads I could take.

I could tell you how all my money is stuck in nonperforming investments but how I need twenty thousand dollars urgently for my poor dear mother's life-saving operation and how I will pay you back, not just in cash but in kind, the kind which you have never experienced before.

You, believing you are Sir Galahad or Sir Lancelot, rush to my rescue by transferring twenty thousand dollars to the bank account number I gave you, dreaming of all the ways you are going to claim your reward.

Or,

I could tell you how I am travelling at the moment in a third world country which has these bad, nasty men and how I am stuck in the Customs where one such bad nasty man will not let me leave unless I give him twenty thousand dollars in Apple gift cards.

You, believing that you are Clark Kent or Bruce Wayne, act swiftly and decisively by purchasing the requisite number of gift cards so that you can release me from the clutches of those evil villains who have imprisoned me in their lair.

Or,

I could go on and on. I am sure you get the gist.

So, that is catfishing.

Based on my limited understanding of James Hong, I decided that catfishing would be the first line of offence.

It is easy. It is proven to be effective. It is reasonably anonymous.

However, my goal was not to extract money from James.

It was to extract James from his life.

So, the next morning after our family dinner, I woke with the familiar stirring in my body. A melange of energy and excitement, with a sprinkling of nervousness.

I let sleeping Nysa lie, brushed, washed, donned my

running gear and set out. The dinner had been, as usual, over the top. My stomach was still taut. I am a glutton, both for food and punishment.

I had the food, now it was time for the punishment.

I ran straight down Bukit Timah Road to Evans Road, turned left, ran past the Botanical Gardens, emerged onto Napier, turned right into Holland, and reached the Green Corridor.

I checked to see if my mid-section showed an inclination to concavity.

It had, partially.

I walked down the Green Corridor back to Bukit Timah Road and from there to the Botanical Gardens MRT. There I resumed running and returned home, drenched but optimally concave.

After a wash I joined Nysa for a light breakfast.

"I've sent you the e-mails that Randall and I have exchanged," she said. "I need to respond to him soon, so please go through them and give me your thoughts."

I told her I would and went to the study.

I opened my laptop and clicked on a file that you wouldn't find in the average laptop.

You remember I told you about how, some years ago, I had made a bargain with a young IT genius? He had knowledge about computer technology and the internet that I knew would help me differentiate myself from fellow CEOs. I had the access to networks and markets that would help him scale up his first business venture. After we shook hands on the deal, Hari spent three months after office hours transferring to me his proficiency in trawling the murky depths of the internet that were not accessible to most people.

One of his lessons was on how to spot a catfisher. To do that, you need to know the mechanics of catfishing – how you use fake data to set up a social media account, how you populate that account to make it seem that it is legitimate and has many connections, how you obtain views and likes for your feed and posts. And how to do all this in a few hours.

The file that I clicked on lit up the path to setting up an untraceable social media account.

Between 9:45 am and 12:30 pm, I became Serena Woo.

I was 31 years old.

My profile picture crooned 'girl next door, but hotter than the usual'.

My feed showed that I lived in a two-bed apartment in a condo and drove a Toyota Camry: comfortable, but not rolling in money.

My posts displayed photos from Bali, Santorini and Ireland.

I was single, but keen on changing that status. I wanted, no, I needed a protector.

I loved fashion, wellness products, food and malls.

In music, there was nothing in the world better than K-Pop. That RM was so dreamy!

I was clueless about economics, politics, finance or anything really material.

All in all, I was a naïve, almost over-the-hill waif seeking an older and wiser Prince Charming.

I let that simmer on the burners and opened Nysa's mail. She and the author had been corresponding for about four days now. I started with the first message from the publisher making the introduction and read through the trail chronologically. The e-mails included Nysa's minutes of their calls. I finished reading and then re-read the whole exchange again.

When I was done, I sat there for a few minutes. I needed to calm myself.

William Randall may have been a best-selling author, but he was not a very nice person. He sounded like an entitled diva. The tone of his messages conveyed that Nysa should feel honoured for even being considered for the role. That it was her privilege to serve him.

When I felt sufficiently serene, I shut the laptop and went to the dining room.

Just after lunch, I started 'liking' various posts, including three on James' feed, where he had posted photos of himself with a couple of colleagues at The Lantern and at Sky Bar.

At around 3:00 pm, I commented on one of his posts about his visit to the Bulgari Store in Paragon. I used more emojis than anybody should.

I left the realm of social media and went back to Nysa's e-mails. I re-read them to make sure that I wasn't missing or assuming anything. Some of Randall's phrases took me back to my sales days, especially to one arrogant customer who thought he could push me around because I needed his company's business more than he wanted our products.

Power corrupts, I thought. It didn't matter if you were a manager or an author; the moment you had what you thought was an upper hand, you flexed your muscle. Humans are so predictable.

I shut down my laptop and went to take a much-deserved

siesta. I woke at 5:30 pm and went to the kitchen to brew a cup of tea for Nysa. She has grown used to such service over the years.

When I returned with her mug, she was sitting up against the headboard and scanning through her messages.

"Thank you, dearest," she said, speaking breathlessly and batting her eyelashes.

I smiled, puffed up my chest and felt chivalrous.

I had been catfished by Nysa many decades before it became a crime.

I went to the study and opened my laptop. There was a message from James Hong on my social media feed.

I clicked on it.

It was a 'friend' request.

CHAPTER 7

I clicked on "Accept".

James and Serena were now friends. Hooray!

I went into his feed. I saw two new posts, one with him in a convertible with a friend and the other holding up a bottle of what I assumed was an expensive, pretentious wine.

I 'liked' both posts and sprinkled more emojis.

I really hoped I was using the right emojis. Other than the basic emotions, I was unable to decipher what most of them signified. I tried to limit myself to using emojis which I saw other women use. There was one that looked appallingly like a raised middle finger, so I avoided that. For now.

Fifteen minutes passed. I refreshed my screen.

James had 'liked' my emoji-laden comments.

I smiled. The bait was in the water and beckoning.

This next part is for those of you for whom digital technology is oil to your water.

There are ways to find out who is looking at your Facebook profile and feed. It is not difficult, only a little cumbersome. If you are interested, you can open Google and type in, 'How to find out who is looking at your

Facebook profile".

I clicked on the appropriate keys.

James had visited my profile four times.

(There are also ways to ensure that if someone is trying to find out if you visited their profile, you could mask yourself. They will not see your visit. That's what I had done when I visited James' profile – masked all my visits but one.)

I carefully drafted my first real message.

'Such a pretty car!" I breathed. "You are so lucky!" I batted.

 More emojis.

As I was waiting for his response, Nysa called.

"Ishmael, are you up for an evening walk? I would like to go to Plaza Singapura."

I looked at the laptop screen. It was time to give James some space.

I changed into my walking clothes and went to the living room.

We left our condo and started walking to Plaza Singapura. Nysa loves this mall. How it is different from any other mall, I haven't the faintest idea. It has the exact same shops in nearly the exact same configuration.

"Shall we discuss the e-mails you sent me?" I asked.

"Of course, Ishmael," said Nysa, "what did you think?"

"From the e-mails," I said, "it sounds like Randall feels that, because he is a best-selling author, he can dictate the terms of the engagement. His approach indicates that you would benefit more than he does from your association with him. The question is whether you are willing to accept his premise or not."

"He does come across as quite arrogant, doesn't he?"

said Nysa, wryly, "but he is a great author, and I would like to work with him. Having him in my client list will also enhance my profile in the publishing world."

"Why is he looking for a change?" I asked, "especially if his first book in the trilogy did so well?"

"I spotted at least eleven factual errors in the book," said Nysa, "and I am sure Randall's critics would have roasted him over the coals for them. He probably wants someone who is more rigorous, I think."

"That's interesting," I responded, "in which case, he needs someone of your calibre more than you need him, and you need to make sure he knows that. So, you need to play a little hardball. But, if you do, you need to be willing to walk away from this contract. Are you okay to do that?"

Nysa hesitated.

"I don't get offers like this often, Ishmael," she said, diffidently, as we walked into the mall, "if this doesn't work out, I will be stuck where I am, working with regional or first-time authors. I was thinking that it would be better to accept his terms this time around. It's not ideal, but…"

"I understand, Nysa," I said, dodging a well-built matron carrying multiple bags, "but if you accept his terms, it is going to establish the tone of the partnership, which is that he is in control, and you are his chattel. It is not likely to be pleasant."

"So, what should I do?" she asked, as we walked past Spotlight, one of Nysa's go-to stores, "what would you do? I need to respond by 10:00 am tomorrow morning."

"The first thing I would do is not reply by tomorrow morning," I said, "so far, you have been eager and responsive. That may have led him to believe that you will concede to his demands. Let's keep quiet and wait till lunchtime. Let's play the staring game for a few hours and see if he blinks."

"And if he doesn't?" asked Nysa, practically, "what if he finds someone else?"

"I will back you in whatever you do, Nysa," I said, "but what I have learnt is that if there is the possibility of a serious imbalance in a relationship, it is best not to enter the relationship at all. Remember what happened with Paloma's start-up?"

Paloma was Nysa's cousin's daughter. She had moved to Singapore two years ago to set up a software services company. When she first moved, Paloma stayed with us for a couple of months. In her desire to grow her start-up rapidly, Paloma entered into an agreement with a large regional reseller. Nysa and I had advised her against this step.

"They are large and powerful, Paloma," Nysa had said, "and you are small and vulnerable. It is not an equitable partnership."

But Paloma was confident that the partnership would help her scale. She thanked us for our advice and went ahead anyway. The reseller set punitive terms. They had unreasonable demands. They took up all of Paloma's bandwidth to the point that she could not service any of her other customers. Six months later, she ended up selling her company to the reseller for a pittance and moved back to the UK.

Nysa was silent for a while.

"I see where you are coming from," she said, "if I don't set the right tone from the beginning, Randall will expect me to be at his beck and call, and I won't be able to give time to my other clients. That wouldn't be fair to them."

We exited the mall and started walking back.

"We will find a way to make this happen," I said, with more confidence than warranted. Nysa tucked her hand in mine. I hoped I was not letting her down.

"I'll draft a response for you," I continued, "which we will send to Randall after his follow-up message or after lunch, whichever comes first."

On returning to the apartment, I changed after a quick wash and closeted myself in the study.

I (breathlessly) opened the laptop and logged into my catfishing avatar.

James had replied to my message. With a private message.

"Life is about enjoyment," he had written. I had no idea he was a philosopher. "Cars, food and fun are my passion! What about you?" His use of emojis was not as considerable as mine.

I put Nysa and her e-mails out of my mind.

To be a good catfisher, you have to become your persona.

I calmed my mind and tried to reduce my IQ by 75%.

"Oh, you are so wise," I gushed. "I, too, love food. And shopping. Not to mention K-Pop."

I made sure I used all the infantile abbreviations that make for social media English nowadays. I also continued to be liberal with the free stock of emojis that Facebook had given me.

His response was almost immediate.

"Oh, love shopping lots!" he wrote, "my favourite places are Paragon and Ion."

Paragon and Ion are upscale shopping malls on Orchard Road. They are large, fancy and places to be seen at and mentioned in social media posts.

I was trying my best to keep in character. But when one sees a thirty-six-year-old man talk about 'fave malls', one feels like slapping said man on the back of his head and ordering him to straighten out.

"Oh, I loooove Metro," I bleated, "what an amazing lingerie collection!" I looked for and found emojis that represented lingerie.

Silence.

Oh God, had I come on too strong? Too soon? Who knew what the mating rituals were nowadays?

I waited. Breathlessly.

Two minutes. Five minutes.

Ding.

"Never been to Metro," he wrote, "Will go this weekend."

I smiled and simpered in emojis.

"Got to go for dinner," I texted, "Chat soon!"

James serenaded me with his emojis.

The screen looked like it had been invaded by buttercups. Yellower than the Huang He River.

I showered him right back.

If we had continued, Facebook would have run out of emojis, so I stopped.

I logged out and shut down the laptop.

Phase 1 – complete. Baited and hooked.

Phase 2 – reel him in. Slowly and carefully.

I got up and went to ask Nysa if she wanted a glass of wine.

She smiled and said yes, making me feel almost heroic.

Pavlov had nothing on me.

CHAPTER 8

Motive, Opportunity and Means.

You must surely have heard of these three words used often in crime dramas and detective serials. It is a popular summation of what it takes for anyone to commit a crime.

True.

First, one needs a motive – a reason to commit the crime.

Then, one requires the opportunity – adequate chance(s) to commit the crime.

Finally, one has to have the means – the ability and tools necessary to commit the crime.

Actually, these three words apply to almost everything we do in our lives.

They tell us why we work.

Our motive – to not starve; the opportunity – the job market; the means – our knowledge, skills, diligence, willingness.

They tell us why we men marry or enter into a long-term relationship;

Our motive – to have access to regular sex; the opportunity – the infinite field of women making themselves available through various channels or on various platforms; the means – our ability to present ourselves as what women want to see and believe.

Basically, for every action we have taken, we can work backwards and identify a motive, an opportunity and a set of means.

And for those actions we have yet to take, such as the case of the planned termination of James Hong, we have to work forwards and develop these.

The motive came from James himself. He was the direct cause of the sequence of events that led to Greg Closier's demise. He contributed to the passing of Lee Sun Wah. He was hurting Marianna's feelings and chances for promotion. James had crossed the line and deserved to be punished.

The opportunity was being developed through 'Serena Woo', my alter ego. As the Facebook 'friendship' evolved, a time would come when Serena would ask James to meet, and that would allow me the chance to meet and confront James.

The means needed thought.

To choose the appropriate tools to use in my forthcoming meeting with James, I would have to first evaluate when and where the meeting was likely to be.

There were, as I saw it, three probable choices.

The first was in a mall, given that both parties seemed to like shopping.

The second was at a restaurant, given the inclination to take pictures of every meal and share it with the world and its uncle.

The third was at a park or garden, given that such locations were the norm for men and women to meet and get to know one another.

There are other possibilities, including James' apartment, a hotel room, a club, and so on, but based on the current information, these were less likely.

Of the three choices, I would prefer a park or garden, preferably in the late evening. Lack of people and lack of light – what is not to like?

But I have to prepare for the worst – for hordes of people and banks of light if the meeting happens in a mall.

I must confess that I had been spending some time on the internet looking at a few alternatives.

We had just finished dinner, and I had left Nysa watching a new Netflix limited series on sugar confections.

I was back in the study and thinking about means.

First, I liked the idea of poison.

Yes, I am aware that poison is considered a woman's weapon, or even a coward's weapon.

I am reasonably secure in my masculinity and my self-image that I don't have to concern myself with such perceptions.

Poison is elegant. It is suave. It persuades the victim to die rather than bludgeons them to death.

However, poison is not user-friendly. It is a double-edged weapon and can as much harm the perpetrator as the victim.

It was also, especially in Singapore, very hard to find without being found out.

Unless one was creative.

I had a few ideas that I was exploring.

Next, I also liked the idea of sharp objects such as ice picks.

They are easy to carry, quick to use, and don't leave much of a mess.

They are widely available in most kitchens and DIY shops.

They are also easy to make from every-day objects, and very easy to dispose.

However, it can be difficult to explain why one is carrying around a very obvious weapon.

Here, too, I was considering some Avant Garde ideas.

Finally, I liked the idea of engineering an accident.

A fatal fall, perhaps, ideally from a high-rise building.

A hit-and-run, late in the night.

An accidental drowning in a bathtub.

However, these methods required a degree of isolation to prepare the scene and persuade the victim to cooperate with one's desires.

Also, one needed to be careful about depositing one's DNA at inconvenient junctures leading to unpleasant discussions with the police.

This option was the least likely, I believed.

But everything was on the table, as the phrase goes.

As I leaned back in my chair, so many cliches from my time at work ran through my mind.

"Proper planning prevents poor performance."

"Failing to prepare is preparing to fail."

"Success is where preparation and opportunity meet."

But the quote I liked best was that of Abraham Lincoln's

—

"Give me six hours to chop down a tree and I will spend the first four sharpening the axe."

Mr. Lincoln was absolutely right.

Much of the success I have seen and encountered in the corporate world came from the ability to plan and prepare.

It was not the most knowledgeable who succeeded.

It was rarely the smartest that prevailed.

It was never those who boasted of any unique talents.

The person who succeeded, always, was the best prepared person in any room. In every situation.

When you are the best prepared, you are able to respond and react faster and better than anyone else. You have more options at hand. You have more tools in your kit.

So, you quickly gain a reputation of having a cool head, of being a calm port in any storm, of thoughtful and adaptive leadership.

People respect that. Subordinates look up to you. Peers turn to you. Superiors depend on you.

Now, you are the go-to person.

Soon, you will go to the corner office, where you will sit behind a humongous desk and in a five-thousand-dollar ergonomic chair.

If I wanted to succeed as an assassin, I would have to draw on all these learnings. I did not have the support systems that I had as a CEO – deputies and managers and secretaries and admin staff. I was alone.

I would need to plan with even more thought and precision.

I would need to evaluate and prepare for all eventualities.

No door could remain unopened, no room could stay unexplored, no option could afford to be overlooked.

Patience.

Adaptability.

Resilience.

I had a lot of learning to do.

It was exciting.

I wanted to continue, but I had promised Nysa a draft response. I opened her e-mail trail and read through the exchanges once again. Then, I started typing.

Dear Mr. Randall,

This has reference to our e-mail exchanges and telephonic discussions over the past few days.

Thank you for offering me the opportunity of working with you. You are an amazing author and your latest book, "Tears of the Land" is, in my opinion, one of the best books that I have had the pleasure of reading in the historical fiction genre.

While I am seized of the privilege that this opportunity offers, it is with regret that I inform you that I am unable to accept the terms and conditions that you have shared with me. They are neither commercially nor contractually viable.

I wish you all the best and look forward to working together in the future.

Warm regards,

It is said that a little flattery goes a long way. But, in this case, not as far as a firm refusal. Divas don't like to be told no. They are like bullies – they have contempt for the ones who flinch, and respect for the ones who stand firm. Randall would not walk away. Okay, scratch that. The probability of Randall walking away was low. He would be intrigued at being so summarily dismissed.

At least, that's how it worked in the corporate world. Writers could have entirely different operating systems and world views. I hoped I was not leading Nysa down the wrong path.

I crossed my fingers and shut down the laptop. It was

time for bed.

When Nysa has wine, it opens up possibilities that must be seized.

INTERLUDE 3

As Ishmael Dollah evaluated diverse approaches to termination, wrote strong e-mails and anticipated having sex with his wife,

Inspector Julia Binti Shafiq sat alone at a table in the Tiong Bahru market food court.

She had a bowl of cooling Laksa in front of her, which she was desultorily dipping into whenever she noticed it.

What was taking most of her attention were the lists that she had next to the bowl.

Lists of Club members who had registered their presence on the night that Greg Closier died.

The Club had three restaurants connected to the main lobby.

One hundred and sixty-nine members and guests had passed through those restaurants between 7:00 pm and 9:00 pm that night.

The closest was The Olde Tavern. Fifty-five members and ten guests.

The next was The Fireplace. Forty members and two guests.

The third was The Tiffin Room. Fifty-one members and eleven guests.

Julia was trying to identify the three images on the security camera video and correlate them to the lists.

The short dark person who followed Greg Closier into the restroom.

The older fair person who exited the restroom next.

The lady who left The Olde Tavern restaurant in the same time frame.

Strangely, none of them seemed to have swiped their card in any of the three outlets. Her team had pulled out the database of members and compared it against the three lists and reliably identified all but these three.

Then, her team had met and questioned the staff from each of the restaurants, but no one could throw any light on these three visitors.

The manager, Kumar, had had a plausible explanation.

"Madam, often members come here to meet other members or guests and either use the lobby or the Verandah. If they don't order any food or drink, they remain outside the system," he explained earnestly and not without a little concern.

Julia picked up her chopsticks and spoon and dipped into the Laksa. It was cold and congealing. She kept the utensils down and pushed aside the bowl.

The short man and the woman had both seemingly come from The Olde Tavern. What were they doing there if they had not eaten or drunk?

The manager had solved that quickly.

"Madam, they may have come with another Club member, who swiped his card," he clarified.

But both of them seemed to have been alone. There was no one accompanying them. And no one amongst the restaurant staff could confirm that either of them were guests at another member's table.

"Or, madam, they may have stepped in, had some water, or asked about the menu or take out, and left," the manager had said, most unhelpfully.

Julia was getting frustrated.

The NSCS people had not come back to her with enhanced images from the piss-poor video, even after she had pulled enough strings to fly a kite.

The staff in the Club seemed to have explanations for everything, except who the three persons of interest were.

Her boss was increasingly unhappy about the time she was taking on this case and the lack of progress.

Most importantly, Julia was frustrated by the feeling that there was something in her peripheral vision, but every time she turned, it disappeared.

There was a connection between the two cases. She knew it. It was tantalising and just out of reach. And come hell or high water, she was going to find it.

She rose and walked to the Kopi Tiam stall to get herself tea. She stood behind a middle-aged lady who was ordering something to go. A few moments later, the lady stepped aside, and the shop keeper gestured to Julia.

"One Teh-C, please", said Julia, "and by the way, what language were you just speaking?"

"Bisaya, madam," said the shopkeeper, "the lady is a domestic helper from the Philippines."

Oh, shit, I was supposed to go and check out the report on the abused maid at Choa Chu Kang, thought Julia. I had time this morning, but it completely slipped my mind. The rest of today is crazily busy. Also, I didn't hear any updates, so maybe it was a false alarm?

She carried her tea cupping the glass in in both hands and went back to the table.

She would go tomorrow. Surely. What could happen in one day?

CHAPTER 9

Friday morning dawned too early.

I was loathe to leave the bed.

The wine last night had worked its wonders on Nysa, who then had worked her wonders on me.

I just wanted to lounge and loll.

Nysa was already up and about.

Sex seems to have very different impacts on us.

It relaxes me.

It energises Nysa.

She must be in the kitchen, I thought, trying out a new recipe. Or in her study, researching some exotic topic for one of her authors.

Knowing that in either case, I was the most likely guinea pig, I thought it best to spend some time in the great outdoors.

I rose, washed, changed and walked to the kitchen to have my daily ration of water.

True enough, Nysa was in the kitchen with Siti, standing in front of a bowl with an unidentifiable concoction in it.

She looked up and smiled.

"Good morning, dearest," she smiled, lighting up the room, "Slept well?"

"Oh yes," I replied, going to her and giving her a kiss. "Off for my run now."

"Oh, would you like to try this," she said, pointing at the bowl, "I am trying a new walnut paste dessert recipe."

Now that I was closer to the bowl, I wanted no part of it. Nysa was an amazing chef, and she would ensure that the walnut paste would be to die for, but not this attempt.

"Not right now, darling," I said, as regretfully as I could, "I won't be able to run."

"Okay," she sighed, both of us playing our roles. "Come back soon."

I finished my glass of water.

"See you, sweetheart. Just let me know if you hear from Randall."

I left the condo and turned left.

Now that the languor had left me, I knew where I wanted to go, and what I needed to do.

Singapore has these wonderful community gardens. Hundreds of them.

Anyone can ask for and be allocated a small plot in such a garden which they can use to grow what they desire.

Not cannabis. Or poppy.

Two months ago, Nysa and I had walked past one of these gardens. Nysa loves plants and flowers, and naturally we entered the gardens and we oohed and aahed about the plants and shrubs that abounded.

Singaporeans being who we are, each pot or patch was meticulously labelled.

Some of the names were interesting and some were

downright catchy.

I have a decent memory and could recall the stickier ones.

A week after that walk, I happened to read a little known crime novel set in a small town in the US where a series of unexplained and unrelated deaths took place. The deaths were a mystery till the CDC came into town and investigated. They quickly and efficiently found the cause.

The CDC found that the town florist had found a new crop of flowers in the nearby woods and added them to the bouquets and arrangements she was selling. The flowers were pretty. They were also pretty deadly. Needless to say, the florist paid for her ignorance with her life, which was a fair trade. Sadly, three of her clients also died, which was a shame, given that they were blameless.

I had seen the name of those flowers before.

In Singapore. In a community garden.

I ran steadily and forty minutes later, entered the small verdant piece of land.

There were four people already there, tending to their plants. They were surrounded by watering cans and spray cans and bags of chemicals and fertilizers. I could hear snatches of conversation extolling the virtues of one product over another, or the vices of an especially reluctant plant.

I walked around, spiralling towards where I had seen the little bush labelled, "Friar's Cap".

I reached the little patch.

And my heart fell.

Evidently, in the last few weeks, someone had had a change of mind. The patch was bursting with green tomatoes and purple eggplant.

No deadly blue flowers.

I walked carefully around the garden, just in case I had missed the precise location of the patch.

No luck. A multitude of flowers and vegetables, but boringly safe.

I looked around to see if there was anyone in charge whom I could ask questions of, but this was a community garden, not a cult.

Okay. That is how the cookie crumbles, sometimes.

I exited the garden and continued my run past Mount Rosie into Chancery Lane and towards Novena.

As my body kept the pace that my aging legs and lungs allowed, my mind slipped into high gear.

The easy way out was blocked.

I would most likely have to acquire Friar's Cap from outside Singapore. There are ways to obtain these in Singapore, but these are restricted and governed by pharmacological regulations.

One of the many positive outcomes of being a CEO is that one develops an amazing network of contacts. Of acquaintances, associates, agents, friends all over the world. If one is a smart CEO, these connections are personal, are kept warm, and don't wither when the position is vacated.

I had, over the course of my career, built such a network. It was not vast, but it was versatile.

Many networks are blinkered – in that they are useful in a limited milieu. For example, a banker's network may be limited to experts and players in the finance domain, but with very limited knowledge or reach into the shipping domain, for instance.

My connections were more eclectic. This was because

my network grew from my likes rather than my needs. I did not make connections for purposes of future use; I had made friends because I liked them and enjoyed interacting with them.

As I ran, I mentally scanned my contact list, especially those in Asia.

Why Asia?

Because, since time unknown, the roots and tubers of Friar's Cap have been used in traditional Indian and Chinese medicine. The plant itself is not native to Asia but is imported in large and regular quantities.

I just needed to get hold of 50 grams.

Another thought occurred to me – that I could also ask for the extract rather than the root. It would be a little difficult to explain, but that is the advantage of having a trusted network, that one did not have to explain oneself too much.

By the time I turned into the road leading to our condo, I had shortlisted two names who I believed could help me with obtaining Friar's Cap – either the root or the extract, or both.

The mild sense of disappointment that had struck me when I couldn't find what I was looking for in the community garden faded away.

As I stepped into the elevator, I started planning the messages that I would send to my two contacts and the structure of the calls that I would have with them.

One of them was in KL, Malaysia and the other in Kochi, India.

I recognised that I may need to travel to either of these cities if I wanted to pick up the item or find a smart way of importing it without subjecting it to the risk of examination by Customs or similar agencies that pry into others' businesses.

If I needed to travel, I would need to create a fictional customer for my consultancy services and have them invite me for a face-to-face meeting.

Oh, and perhaps I would need to buy some other herbs and/or extracts that would mask my intention. I added this to my call agenda.

I said hi to Nysa. No news from Randall so far. I went to the study and sat at my desk.

I composed the e-mails I needed to send and checked them, revising a couple of small points. The one to KL was easier, as my connection there was someone whom I had known for a long time and trusted implicitly. He lived in a grey world, and I had utilised his unadvertised services many times before. The email to Kochi was a little more convoluted, packed with a list of herbs and extracts, as I was not completely sure of the recipient's discretion.

I reviewed the emails one last time and pressed Send.

Whoosh!

CHAPTER 10

Once that was done, I logged into Facebook as Serena Woo.

It was more than twelve hours since Serena and James had bid goodbye to one another, and absence was a powerful force.

As soon as the main feed filled the laptop screen, I saw that James was very keen on continuing the conversation.

"Hi, Serena," was his first message.

"Great talking to you last night," was his second.

Some photos of himself in a bar followed.

"Wish you were here," was next.

One point of order. From the above series of messages, it may read like a sane, rational dialogue.

It was not.

Young people seem to have the innate ability to mangle language to the point of incomprehension. There were more acronyms and abbreviations than I had learnt jargon in my entire career.

BTW. LOL. BRB. TTYL. LMK. SMH. NVM.

While I had to read only a few 'sentences', I had to refer to the internet at least eight times to try and figure out what James was saying and why.

If that was not bad enough, I had to now compose my responses and then change them into the gobbledegook that passed for communication nowadays.

If I failed in my catfishing, it would be because I was too old for this juvenile crap.

I carefully planned my responses.

Then I went back into the internet and did my best to translate my sentences into a form that James would understand and accept.

What I said was –

"Hi James."

"Great to connect with you."

"I had fun last night chatting with you."

"Where is this bar? It looks cool."

"What is your plan for this weekend?"

You do not want to see what I actually wrote.

I couldn't decipher it myself.

I left the laptop on and went to the dining room to join Nysa for breakfast.

Today we were having yoghurt, fruit and Christmas cake.

Yes, I agree that that was a strange combination.

You will recall that I told you about Nysa and her talents. One of them was baking cakes. Not just cakes, every form of baked creation – rolls, muffins, baguettes, croissants, pies, tarts, brownies, blondies – you name it, and she could bake it and you would sell your firstborn for it.

While she has an innate gift, perfection comes from practice.

Nysa practices all the time. You will agree that this is truly commendable – the dedication, the focus, the diligence. All these are qualities I have looked for and rarely found in the corporate world.

But. Even silver linings have clouds.

Nysa practices on me.

You frown. Why is this a problem, dude, you ask. Shouldn't you be happy getting a regular supply of free cakes and muffins and brownies and cookies, you say.

Well, you are mostly right.

Till you remember the concept of evolution.

It took millions of years for a man to evolve from an ape. For prehensile tails to change to opposable thumbs. From scampering on all fours to standing erect.

Cakes (and other baked goods) go through a similar process of evolution.

When first baked, they tend to be dense. They collapse. They char. They sometimes tend to be chewier than gum. Often, they are harder than igneous rock. I have even seen them crumble when a door slams in another part of the building.

It is only over time that they begin to evolve into the airy, fluffy, sugary delights that they should be.

Nysa is also a good hostess.

She understands that guests must be treated with courtesy. And hospitality. And must never be exposed to the dark underbelly of the baking world.

So, when I sit at the dining table and am served Christmas cake, I know that it is not going to be that rich, rum-filled, fruity, moist, heavenly creation that you immediately assume when you hear the words, "Christmas cake".

I know that it is more likely to be something that.

a, I will find difficult to chew or swallow, and

b, that will cast my insides into violent disorder for hours.

I look up in dismay at Nysa.

"See what I made for you!" she exclaims, happily.

I sit down at the table with the same enthusiasm that a man exhibits before entering a room for his prostrate exam.

The yoghurt was creamy and tangy.

The watermelon was fresh and sweet.

The Christmas cake was not something the Magi would have enjoyed. In fact, if they were offered it, they may have taken their gifts back with them.

However, I have learnt from bitter (pun intended) experience not to discuss Nysa's creations without using positive superlatives.

So, I lied through my teeth.

Given that my teeth were firmly welded together by a product that 3M would love to patent, it was the only thing I could do.

"Exceptional," I gritted, "Exquisite."

I could only use words that did not need my opening my mouth more than half a centimetre.

"Thank you, sweetie," Nysa trilled, "I am going to try another batch this afternoon. I will make sure it is ready by breakfast tomorrow."

I swear, sometimes I feel that she enjoys putting me through this perverse ritual.

Picking up a glass of water that I vainly hoped would dissolve the cake in my mouth, I went to the study.

It took about seven minutes for the so-called cake in my mouth to dissolve. That was a definite improvement; a few months ago, Nysa had tried out an Indian sweet, 'basin ladoo', that glued my mouth shut for more than an hour.

As I worked my jaw muscles, I looked at my watch.

Time to resume Serena's dalliance with James.

In the time that I had had breakfast, James had been quite voluble

It was almost 10:30 am. It was a working day. Did he have nothing to do? No briefs to write, no people to sue, no depositions to conduct?

I sat down and started deciphering his comments.

As I struggled with the acronyms, my phone pinged. It was Nysa.

'E-mail from Randall, have forwarded it to you'

I took a break from James and switched over to Outlook. I opened the e-mail.

Hi Nysa,

As discussed, I was expecting to receive your email confirming your acceptance.

Please confirm at the earliest.

Randall.

I picked up my laptop and walked to Nysa's study. She was at her desk. She looked up at me.

"So?" she asked.

I opened the e-mail I had drafted and showed it to her. She read it twice.

"What do you think?" I asked.

"Isn't it a little too abrupt?" said Nysa, frowning, "will he get offended?"

"Nysa, you will be working on this book with Randall for at least twelve months," I said, "you are going to disagree with him, you are going to push back, you are going to offer opinions that he may not appreciate. If he is the kind of person who will take offence to honest feedback, isn't it better to know now and walk away?"

Nysa considered my point. She nodded.

"You are right, Ishmael," she said, "this relationship must be on an equal footing. Otherwise, it is not worth the trouble."

I sent the draft to her laptop. She opened it, copied, and pasted it in response to Randall's latest message. She looked once more at me, still not fully sure. Then she pressed 'Send'.

"Thank you, Ishmael," said Nysa.

"Thank me if the ploy works," I said, bending down and kissing her on her forehead. I left her and went back to the study. It was time to resume my discussion with James.

Three minutes later, I leaned back in my chair.

Not good.

James, it seems, did not believe in the slow and steady rhythm of the mating ritual.

James, it seems, was in a hurry. Either he was a man of little patience, or his biological clock was ticking.

He wanted to meet Serena.

Tomorrow.

CHAPTER 11

That was not good, but it was not a serious issue.

One of the primary skills of catfishing was to be able to keep the victim on the line for extended periods.

Making them believe that things are going to happen that never will.

Most catfishers never meet their victims.

They promise to.

They set up dates and times and trysts.

They express their desperate desire to 'take the next step'.

But alas.

Something comes up. Something always comes up.

A sudden business trip.

A sick mother.

An unreasonable boss.

And the meeting has to be rescheduled, Postponed.

So near, and yet, always so far.

Does this sound like I am an expert catfisher? That I have done this in the past? That I am experienced and adept?

If it does, I am sorry.

This was my first time.

I am catfishing virgin.

I have read so much about it, in books, newspaper articles, magazines, blogs.

I have also had the dubious honour of knowing a couple of victims who have poured their hearts out to me. Thankfully, they did not realise that, regardless of my sympathetic expression, I was wondering why they were so stupid.

At this juncture, I would like to make two points –

One, you will appreciate that catfishing is only an extension of a con. And cons have been going on for as long as humans have roamed the earth.

A conman, George Parker, sold the Statue of Liberty and the Brooklyn Bridge to idiots.

Another, Michael Corrigan, sold Big Ben and the Tower of London to morons.

A third, Mithilesh Srivastava, sold the Taj Mahal and the Red Fort to simpletons.

Another, Bernie Madoff, bilked his high profile, imbecile clients of fifty billion dollars.

So, catfishing is not new. It is just easier, faster, and much more scalable when done digitally, that's all.

Two, much of marketing and selling in the corporate world is a form of catfishing.

For years, I have been seducing customers by telling them what they want to hear and selling them what I had in stock.

How do we do this?

We build a persona – for ourselves and our company – that fits the image that the customer has in mind of a trustworthy, supportive, caring entity.

We use that persona to inveigle our way into the

customer's office, mind and heart.

We let the customer believe that what we have is exactly what they need and have always wanted.

Then, we make the sale.

When you buy that shampoo that implies that you are going to look like Beyonce once you use it, you have been catfished.

When you buy that car that promises you that you will feel like George Clooney the moment you start driving, you have been conned.

When you buy the apartment that the realtor tells you will make sure everyone knows that you have arrived, you are the latest sucker born.

Points made.

So, was I an experienced catfisher?

No.

Was I experienced in corporate sales?

Yes. Very much.

I spent the next few minutes crafting Serena's message to James.

In it, I expressed my unbridled enthusiasm at the prospect of meeting him in person.

Then, I said that while I had to take care of my ailing grandmother over the weekend, I would surely get away by 4:00 pm on Saturday.

Finally, I suggested a designer shop in a mall where we could meet.

I translated this into millennial-ese and sent it zooming to James.

While I was waiting for his response, I decided to check my e-mail for any responses from my two contacts regarding my request.

"Ishmael," said Nysa urgently, walking into the study. Her phone was buzzing. "It's Randall."

I stood up.

"Ignore it," I said, "let the call ring out."

"But…," said Nysa.

"It's okay, Nysa," I reassured her, "we will call him back."

Nysa stood there looking uncertain. After a few more buzzes, the phone quieted. I gestured to the settee. She sat down. I asked her for the phone and pulled up Randall on WhatsApp.

'Sorry, William, I am on a call, may we speak around 2:00 pm SGT?' I typed and showed the message to Nysa. She nodded. I pressed 'send'.

"Let him stew a little," I said, smiling. Nysa smiled back, but without conviction.

"Now let's plan what we are going to say," I said, "he's going to push, and if that doesn't work, to negotiate. You must be firm about where you are going to draw the line and make a stand. Anything better and you accept the deal. Anything worse and you walk away."

Nysa's phone buzzed.

'Please call at the earliest'

"I believe he is feeling a little stressed," I said, "let's ratchet up the pressure."

I turned to my laptop, opened a new Word document, and started writing out a narrative. I read aloud as I wrote, and Nysa modified and added as we went along. We finished and reviewed what we had written and made some minor changes.

"Are you comfortable with this?" I asked.

"Yes," said Nysa, "it captures exactly what I want to say. I just hope I can say it confidently."

"Do you want me there for the call?" I asked.

"Umm, no, it's okay," said Nysa, getting up to leave, "I'll take care of it. Thanks, Ishmael, you are a sweetheart."

I went back to Outlook to check if there were any responses from KL or Kochi.

Nothing yet.

I opened the browser and started looking for alternate poisons.

Some of them were quite straightforward.

Common pesticides.

Certain drugs.

Cleaning products.

Some of them are a little more exotic.

Tetrodotoxin.

Botulism.

Maitotoxin.

Each of them had, as with most things, their advantages and disadvantages.

The main disadvantage with most of them was that they would be discovered in an autopsy.

An autopsy was likely.

Generally speaking, one does not expect a reasonably healthy person in their thirties to drop dead without cause. So, coroners, before they give their verdict, look for the cause.

In the absence of an obvious bullet wound in the forehead or a knife sticking out of the chest, coroners conduct what is called a toxicology test. They test for substances that should not be present in the body. Arsenic, for example. Or strychnine. Most poisons tended to stick around in the body and wave flags to attract coroners' attention.

When coroners find such a substance, they cry foul. They make a fuss. And the police go on a rampage, throwing extra resources, asking questions of all and sundry, diving into browser histories, watching and rewatching camera feeds.

I was trying to avoid that.

So, I had to find a poison that, when found in the body, did not seem out of place.

I spent the next hour searching the internet and found three prospects that break down into elements that occur naturally. This means that, after an hour or so, there would be no trace of the original chemical in the body. All that the coroner would find is slightly heightened amounts of chemicals found naturally in the body, and thus, not in the least suspicious.

Two of them had a problem – they needed to be injected. Coroners look closely for injection sites. Of course, over the past two years, given the proliferation of vaccines and flu shots, this is less of a problem than it could have been. But, still.

Ideally, the poison needed to be ingestible.

The third fit the bill. Not only was it ingestible, it could only be detected by a gas chromatography or mass spectrometry. While such equipment is commonplace on serials like CSI and NCIS, most real life coroners do not have access to such facilities.

I shut down the browser and deleted the history.

While Nysa and I have a good relationship, I don't want her to come across anything that may make her suspicious of my feelings for her.

Or give her any ideas.

I went back into Facebook.

James had confirmed that he would be there tomorrow at 4:00 pm.

I ensured that Serena said and emojied all the right things.

I logged out.

It was time for lunch.

INTERLUDE 4

As Ishmael Dollah developed expertise in untraceable poisons and arranged a tryst with James Hong,

Inspector Julia Binti Shafiq was both excited and furious.

Excited because Chee Wee had just called her. The enhanced photos from the NSCS had arrived. Finally.

The excitement helped, to an extent, to take her mind off why she was angry.

Julia was infuriated with herself.

She was in Choa Chu Kang, investigating the brutal abuse of an Indonesian helper. The host family had starved the helper. They had prevented her from going out anywhere. They had beaten her, scalded her, kicked her.

The helper, Fatimavati, was in her forties, about 5' 2", and weighed 35 kgs. She was half-dead, terrified and almost catatonic. She was now in the Intensive Care Unit of Tan Tock Seng Hospital.

The 'unofficial' complaint turned out to be agonizingly true.

Why the hell didn't I immediately check this report out? she asked herself. I had two days and didn't do anything.

Perhaps I could have prevented the situation from going so far?

Julia had dealt with many domestic worker abuse cases like this. And each time, she felt sick and frustrated and mad as hell. This time was even worse; she had had a chance to stop it, and she had allowed it to slip.

How can a human being treat another human being like this, she thought.

That, too, someone who is under your care, your protection. Someone who is far away from her home and family, someone who has sacrificed her time with her children to earn money so that she could give them a better life.

The host family, the Soons, consisted of a dominant wife, a henpecked husband and a delinquent adolescent son.

The investigation had just begun, but it was clear that the wife and the son were the main culprits.

They were nasty bits of work. Entitled and arrogant, they showed no remorse.

"She disobeyed me," said Madam Soon, indignantly, "me! I am the one who pays her salary and takes care of her!"

The irony evidently escaped the woman.

"She burnt my Manchester United t-shirt while ironing it," complained Boon Tay, the son, "she deserved to be beaten!"

The husband was a lost cause.

Crushed under years of his wife's berating and bullying, he had very little to say.

"She is a good helper," is all Mr. Soon could manage, "so sorry, madam."

During her investigation, Julia had found evidence of

Fatimavati being tied with rope to her bed.

She also learnt that the helper would be locked inside a wardrobe as punishment for imaginary crimes.

"I also lock my son there!" cried the wife, justifying her action, "it is for their good!"

Julia turned to Investigating Officer Martin Song. She had to leave before she said or did anything that she would regret.

"Could you please finish up here, Martin?" she asked, "I have another case to handle back at HQ."

"No problem, boss," said Martin, "I will come by your office and update you by the end of the day."

Martin was such a great guy to have in the team, she thought.

"Thank you, Martin," Julia said, warmly, and left the ugliness to walk out into the sun.

She walked down to the open car park and got into her car. She sat for a few minutes.

I wish I had come here yesterday or the day before, she thought. I failed Fatimavati. She needed me and I wasn't there for her. How could I do this? she berated herself. I can understand anyone else delaying, but I should have acted immediately.

She looked at the rear-view mirror and saw the dismay in her eyes. She looked away.

Julia started her car. It is this Closier case, she gritted. It is driving me around the bend.

She squealed out of the car park, faster than it was advisable or permissible.

Now, I am going to find out who you are, she thought. You are going to pay.

CHAPTER 12

Lunch was a more palatable affair than breakfast.

To be fair, today's breakfast was the exception rather than the rule.

Lunch was a crunchy salad followed by an amazing risotto and culminating in a chocolate parfait that would have been the envy of the Gods.

I silently forgave Nysa for the Christmas cake.

Over lunch, she told me about her plans for the weekend. She was meeting with some friends for lunch on Saturday and wanted to catch the latest Bond movie on Sunday.

I laid the ground for a possible trip to KL and/or Kochi, weaving a tale of new clients wanting to have kick-off meetings before committing to long term consultancy agreements.

I don't like lying to Nysa, but you have to do what you need to do.

After lunch, Nysa went off to her study to call William Randall. I had e-mailed the narrative that we had drafted for her reference.

I paced the living room for a few minutes. Then I went

out to the balcony to calm my nerves with a soothing application of nicotine.

The cigarette ended too soon. I resume my pacing. I was concerned that Nysa should not allow herself to be bullied. I knew she wanted to work with Randall as he was in the big leagues, but I hoped she would not make too many compromises that she would regret later.

The study door opened, and Nysa stepped out. Her face was flushed. She saw me and smiled victoriously.

"I did it!" she exclaimed, "In the beginning, I stuck to the script and then as the call continued, I realised I didn't need the script. I knew what I wanted and told him that if he if could not accept my terms, I would be happy to find him someone else."

"Good for you, Nysa," I said, happily.

"Twice during the call, he made noises that he would go with someone else," she said, "and I realised I was okay with that, and I told him so, sincerely. He was taken aback, I think."

"After that, his tone changed," she continued, "he tried explaining to me why we would make a good team, and how I could look forward to at least two or three more books. I agreed with him and even suggested a couple of plot points that he could explore. He seemed quite impressed."

"Finally, he said that he will need to discuss this with his agent and the publisher," ended Nysa, with a note of triumph in her voice, "but I am confident that he will come back on our terms."

"That's fantastic, Nysa," I said, and gave her a hug, "well done!"

She hugged me back hard and stepped back.

"Now Siti and I need to go to FairPrice," she said, "I need to replenish some provisions. We will be back in a couple of hours, okay?"

"How many items do you have on your list?" I asked.

"What list?" she replied.

"The list of items that you are going to… oh, it's okay," I sputtered out.

"No one shops with a list, Ishmael," she retorted, closing the conversation.

After they left, I went to the study to check my emails.

The first response had arrived. It was from KL.

Hi, Ishmael, good to hear from you.

Trust all well.

Re your request, I have checked and found a source for the item. Can get it by tomorrow. Is 50 grams sufficient?

Do you want me to courier it? If it is not urgent, I am sending a shipment to Singapore early next week and can add this. It will be with you latest by Wednesday.

When are you in KL next? You owe me a drink!

Cheers…

Aziz.

That was good news.

That is also what I liked about the right kind of friends.

They did not ask questions.

"Why do you want this toxic chemical that can cause disability and death?"

"Are you planning to murder someone?"

They trusted you and were very understanding if you murdered someone. They had also murdered a few people themselves and were not inclined to throw stones.

I dashed off a reply,

Hi, Aziz,

We are good. Thanks for the quick response.

50 gms is more than enough.

No hurry, Wednesday next week is fine.

Let me know the damages.

Re KL, not sure. Perhaps in the next month or two. Nysa has been wanting to go to Ipoh, so…

I owe you many drinks, my friend.

Take care,

Cheers…

I quickly logged on to Facebook to see if there was anything further for Serena from James.

Nothing.

He was probably preparing for his 'date'.

I spent about fifteen minutes being Serena, liking and commenting and posting stuff that would not have any impact.

I had to keep the illusion alive and developing.

That done, I logged out and went back into the internet.

This time, I went into a dark site.

The dark web is a part of the internet that is intentionally hidden. It cannot be reached with regular search engines or browsers, and instead requires the use of specialized software.

I had a little access to this specialised software.

I looked for the ingestible poison I had found earlier.

And the two injectable poisons, too.

All three were available with free shipping.

Though not to Singapore.

I checked if they would ship to KL.

They would.

I looked at their payment requirements and mechanisms. A little different from Amazon, but doable.

I placed a three-day 'no-deposit reserve' on the ingestible poison and received an immediate confirmation. This was just me being anal. I always had to have a back-up plan. In case of the remote possibility that Aziz's consignment was held up in transit. Once I received Aziz's package, I would cancel the reservation.

Logging out, I decided I had earned a cigarette, and went to the balcony.

As I gazed out on the dark clouds forming in the distance, I started planning a timeline.

Assuming I received the package from KL by Wednesday the following week,

I would need another day, or make it two, to prepare it for use. That's Friday.

In which case, Serena could agree to meet James on Saturday.

Where? At what time?

To Be Decided.

If the package was delayed or held up, and either it or the back-up poison arrived by Friday or the weekend, Should I plan a meeting during the work week?

When? Where? At what time?

To Be Decided.

The place had to be one where Serena and James could have a drink or something to eat.

Ideally, it had to be self-service. Or, would it be better if there were wait staff involved?

It needed to be busy.

It shouldn't be too posh.

I stubbed out my cigarette.

Tomorrow, I would list a few prospective locations.

On Monday, I would visit the locations and evaluate them.

As I was leaving the balcony, a thought struck me.

Was I approaching this wrong?

Should I consider a more 'physical' accident? Would that be likelier to believe with a young man, than a sudden collapse in a restaurant?

The problem with this approach was that most places James visited were very public. There would be too many witnesses. And with the number of smart phones out there, a real possibility of being captured for posterity.

I continued thinking of different options as I went to the study.

I would probably need to plan for both options, I thought.

I picked up my iPad, went to our bedroom and sat in the massage chair.

I chose a gentle massage and opened the latest edition of the Economist.

It seemed from the lead article that Vladimir Putin never had to worry about such things as options. Whatever he did was the right option.

CHAPTER 13

"

Ishmael! Where are you?"

I was in the corner of a dimly lit bar.

James was in front of me.

I had just emptied the contents of a sachet into his cocktail and was waiting intently for him to drink.

Just as he picked up the glass, Nysa walked in.

"Ishmael? Where are you, dearest?"

Oh God! What is she doing here?

James looked around, and then back at me.

"Who is she? What does she want?" he asked.

I didn't answer.

He leaned forward and gripped me by the shoulder and shook me.

"Ishmael!"

I startled awake.

I was in the massage chair, iPad in my lap. Nysa was standing next to me, her hand on my shoulder. She seemed amused.

"What?" I asked, a little annoyed.

"Can you be more of a cliché?" she asked, smiling, "an

old man asleep in a massage chair in the afternoon?"

"I didn't plan to fall asleep," I said, defensively, "any way, I am old, and I am allowed to sleep in the afternoon."

"Yes, but it's almost 5:00 pm," said Nysa, "and you know that you will find it difficult sleeping later at night."

I extracted myself from the massage chair.

"Finished your shopping?" I asked as I walked towards the bathroom for a quick wash.

"Yes, all done," she said, "and see what I have got for you!"

I almost groaned.

Nysa's shopping was about 1% planned and 99% impulse.

Too often, her impulses let her to believe that I was in dire need of a particular object. The fact that we had never discussed this, nor had I ever expressed a desire for this object was never the point. The fact that the object was on sale was the only consideration.

"I already have too much stuff, Nysa," I said, as I closed the bathroom door.

"You will love this!" she yelled.

Nysa always likes the last word.

I washed up and went to the dining room where the spoils from the shopping trip were scattered all over.

Siti and Nysa were sorting the items and putting them away into various nooks and crannies.

I went over to help.

As I picked up the case with twenty-four cartons of almond cream (who buys twenty-four cartons of almond cream?) and carried it to the pantry, Nysa opened one of the shopping bags.

"Ta-da!" she exclaimed.

It was an elegant box containing what looked like an armband.

I looked at her.

"It's for your phone," she said, "to carry it when you are running. You can clip it on your arm, so that you have your hands free."

This was actually useful. I opened the box and tried out the armband. I tucked my phone into it. Yes, it was comfortable and easy to access.

"Thank you so much, dearest," I said, "I love it."

She beamed and continued unbagging the nearly two tons of groceries they had bought.

I went to the kitchen, had a drink of water and wandered to the balcony.

That was a strange dream, I thought. Was it some kind of omen? Was the universe sending me a message?

I thought about it for a couple of minutes.

I shrugged. If someone or something is sending me a message, they should make it easier to understand, I told myself. Cryptic isn't my thing. Hints and suggestions are like water off a duck's back. It will need to be something explicit, like – DO NOT KILL JAMES HONG. NOT NOW. NOT EVER.

Till that time, I would continue with my plan.

I went to the study and opened the laptop.

The next topic I needed to research were sharp objects.

Before I proceed, you should know this. The Singapore Government frowns on sharp objects. They frown on many things, but for sharp objects, their frowns are especially deep and scowl like. Singapore has a long list of 'Prohibited Items'. If you are caught in possession of any of these items, they invite you to be their guest for many years in one of their establishments especially designed for this purpose. Prohibited Items included flick knives, butterfly knives, wasp knives, throwing knives, swords, spears, bayonets, daggers, the list goes on and on. I am speaking literally; the list runs to more than forty pages.

So, most knives were taboo. Also, while knives were useful instruments, they were very messy. Or, rather, cutting and slicing was messy. I needed to find a something that was thin, narrow and stabbed deep without causing a bloodbath. Something like an ice pick.

Strangely, the Singapore Government did not object to ice picks.

I looked at ice picks. There were a wide variety available, ranging from 3" picks to 9" picks.

There was a very elegant looking Japanese 'ice knife' which was about 7" long and looked like it meant business.

During my search, I also found some very interesting extrapolations on ice picks.

There were stainless steel martini picks which looked like shiny, lethal knitting needles.

There were steel punch picks which looked as if they could make holes in tank armour.

I found a forged steel marlin spike which spoke to my primal beliefs.

Finally, there was "The Pencil", a steel rod that looked like a pencil, but was actually a sharpened pick or awl use to making holes in a wide variety of media.

All in all, it was enjoyable evening. To paraphrase Churchill, never in the history of mankind has there been so much to kill with, and so few to kill.

I did not purchase anything. Nor did I place anything in a cart.

I would have to find a way to acquire what I needed without traceability. Which meant that someone else would have to buy it, or that I would have to buy it through a cash transaction.

Three of the products – the ice knife, the marlin spike and the Pencil – were available in offline stores. I took down the addresses and the shop timings.

I glanced at the time. It was almost 6:45 pm.

There was time for one more quick search – chemicals and gases.

I quickly glanced through the list of harmful chemicals.

I had always done poorly in chemistry. The names and formulae that the website threw up were like gibberish to me.

I took my time and parsed each suggestion.

Gradually, a couple of interesting candidates emerged.

The first was Ethylene Glycol.

Ethylene Glycol is the main ingredient in anti-freeze and coolant for cars.

Singapore has enough cars to ensure a river of the stuff.

I learnt that in the human body, the alcohol is converted into glycolaldehyde which then oxidises into a substance called oxalic acid which then kills cells. Rapidly.

The advantage is that Ethylene Glycol tastes good and can easily be used in a cocktail with no one noticing the difference.

The second was Potassium Cyanide.

You have surely heard of Potassium Cyanide. Hundreds of people have been killed using this toxic chemical, by

Agatha Christie, Mary Higgins Clark and Dorothy Sayers. It is a colourless crystal, similar in appearance to sugar. It is commonly used in organic synthesis and electroplating. What was interesting is that most jewellers stock this chemical.

Singapore has hundreds of jewellers.

Potassium Cyanide is highly toxic. It inhibits cellular respiration, causing the victim to lose consciousness and leading to brain death.

It scores well in that it is easily dissolved in water, and the slightly acrid taste can be masked with bitters or lemon.

I listed down a couple of places where both Ethylene Glycol and Potassium Cyanide could be purchased. I would need to check them out. Did one need a license to buy these chemicals? Would they want to see identification? Were there restrictions?

Good questions, all.

I shut down the laptop.

Time for dinner.

CHAPTER 14

On Friday nights, usually, Nysa and I walk down to one of the many food courts around us and have a proper Singaporean meal.

This Friday, we walked to 313's food court on Orchard Road, a beautiful, airy space with more than 50 food stalls with cuisines from all over the world.

We found a table and 'choped' it.

Choping is a peculiarly Singaporean custom. It is reserving a table or space by the dint of leaving your wallet or mobile or a handkerchief. Then you go wandering about and when you return, your table will be there for you, even if there are hundreds of people waiting for one.

Singaporeans are a delightful people, for the most part.

We then went hunting.

Nysa prefers Thai or Mediterranean food. I like Laksa and Curries.

We ordered our desires at different stalls, waited, picked up the trays of steaming, aromatic dishes and came back to our table.

My mobile phone sat there undisturbed.

The Olive fried rice was amazing and the Laksa was to die for.

We had also placed an order for desserts, which I went and picked up when we finished our main courses. Nysa had opted for the Pulut Hitam and I went for my usual, the mango boba Chendol. Pulut Hitam is a Malay sweet rice pudding made with coconut milk, palm sugar, pandan and black glutinous rice. It tastes wonderful but has more carbs than I care for. My go-to dessert is always Chendol, and each food court has its own unique version.

As always, while we were dining, we spoke about the children.

Nysa was quite annoyed that they were not populating the world and giving her grandkids.

"They are almost in their mid-thirties, Ishmael," she said earnestly, "by the time I was thirty-five, Shahed was nearly ten years old."

I tried to tell her that things have changed.

"Things have changed, Nysa," I said. I am nothing if not original.

"Both of them are focused on their careers," I continued, "If Marianna gets the Joint Managing Partner job, she will not have time for a child."

That was evidently the wrong thing to say.

"What do you mean?" she asked, quite agitated, scattering the fried rice on the tray. "You mean they will never have children?"

"I am sure they will, when the time is right," I soothed.

"And when will that be?" she asked, "when I am on my deathbed?"

Nysa can be quite melodramatic when the situation calls

for it.

"Also, you are too young to be a grandmother," I said, trying to get the evening back on track.

That brought a semblance of a smile to her face.

"Flatterer," she said, returning to her food.

"By the way, Shahed mentioned that they are planning on buying a house," I said.

"Yes, he told me," Nysa nodded. "They are looking for a penthouse or a landed property. It is likely to be further away, perhaps in Clementi or Siglap."

She did not sound very happy.

"It's only 15 minutes away, sweetheart," I said, "nothing will change."

She pushed away her plate and consoled herself with the dessert.

After the meal, we walked around the mall, identifying the new outlets and trying to recall the ones that had been there and had now bitten the dust.

To our delight, we crossed a new store proudly offering 'Facial Wax Massage". Why didn't people understand the importance of punctuation?

"Do you think Marianna will get the job?" she asked suddenly.

I was taken by surprise.

"Um, I don't know, dearest," I said, "she is an amazing lawyer, and seems to have great client relationships, but I don't know enough about the internal dynamics of Nestor & Ross to be able to make a guess."

"Why do you ask?" I asked curiously.

"I know I want grandchildren, but Marianna must achieve her dreams," she said, "that has to come first."

I told you. Nysa is an absolutely amazing person.

"I agree," I said.

"I hope that colleague of hers she was talking about does not spoil things for her," she said, a little angrily, "I know it happened to you in Axxon, when that stupid Param spread rumours about you…"

That took me back almost twenty-five years. I had mostly forgotten.

I was in my mid-thirties and rising rapidly in my career.

The Chief Operating Officer, who was my boss, was retiring. I was very keen on taking over from him. I was the Head of Department - Logistics at that time. I was not the most senior candidate in the running, but I was doing well and had accumulated a fair share of visible successes.

The CEO and a couple of Board members had met with me. One of them had even hinted that I was the favoured candidate.

Being my usual optimistic self, I thought it was in the bag. I was excited and thrilled.

I was also being my usual unempathetic, blind self.

One of the other contenders for the role, Param Mendes, who was the VP – Technical, sensed the situation veering away from him. He then started a rumour that I was taking money from my vendor partners and steering business to them.

I had absolutely no idea this was happening. When it came to politics, I was always the last person to know, that too, only when one of my colleagues took pity, sat me down, and updated me.

A couple of weeks later, the CEO called me and informed

me that the role was going to someone else.

I was devastated.

I asked him why.

He hemmed and hawed and said that 'you are not ready yet' and that the Board had opted for experience.

I was terrible at reading people, but even I knew that something was rotten in Denmark.

I sought answers and found them. But it was too late.

I remember sitting with my head in Nysa's lap and crying. I remember her consoling me, alternating between sorrow and anger.

I had wanted to quit the next day.

Nysa advised me against doing so.

"If you leave now," she said, wisely, "everyone will believe that the rumours were true. You need to stay, repair the damage, and then give them the finger."

She was right.

I went back to work. With a vengeance.

One of the first things I did was to form an independent committee of my peers, including Param, to review and vet all vendor contracts, and audit the relationships on behalf of Axxon. I ensured that I stayed away.

It took seven months. The committee confirmed that they would not recommend any changes to the vendors. They also confirmed that the due diligence performed, and the audits carried out were above reproach.

It was a fine Wednesday morning when I handed over their report to the CEO. I personally handed a copy to each of the Directors.

Then I submitted my resignation.

Pandemonium ensued.

For one, the new COO was entirely out of his depth and was presiding over one screw-up after another.

Secondly, the Board had already received advance copies of the committee report and had recognised that they had made an erroneous decision based on unsubstantiated information.

Over the next 2 weeks, I was breakfasted, lunched and dined.

I ate, drank, smiled.

Then I left.

"…you see that? That was where Skechers was!" Nysa was saying.

I pulled myself back to the present.

"Yes, I remember," I said, "when did they move out?"

I took her hand in mine.

Marianna was different. She was made of more pliable stock than I. If she was not offered the Managing Partner role, she would accept it and continue working. She would compromise rather than confront.

I would not allow petty jealousy to hurt Marianna's chances, I promised myself. James would not do to Marianna what Param did to me.

Even though I triumphed in the end, I still remember the hurt and pain I felt when the CEO told me that I had been rejected by the Board.

Never again.

INTERLUDE 5

As Ishmael Dollah completed his trip down memory lane while he and Nysa were walking through the mall,

Inspector Julia Binti Shafiq and her technician Chee Wee were sitting in the conference room which they had booked earlier.

The long table was littered with a few 8" x 10" photos.

Chee Wee had spent the early afternoon printing out every file that NSCS had sent and had numbered them.

In front of Julia, on her left was a slowly growing pile of photos that she deemed relevant.

On one of the chairs was a larger pile of discards.

They had fallen into a rhythm. Chee Wee would call out a number and the time the photo was taken. He would pass it on to Julia. She would scan it and decide if it needed to go into the 'relevant' pile or the 'discard' pile.

They were reaching the end.

Chee Wee passed on the next photo to Julia.

She looked at it.

Her breath caught.

She kept it in front of her and pulled the topmost photo

from the relevant pile.

She kept the two photos side by side and her eyes flitted from one to the other.

"Chee Wee," she said, her voice urgent, "please stay in this room and do not move. Do not allow anyone inside."

She got up and walked rapidly to the door and thence to the third floor where her temporary office was.

She unlocked it, went in and opened the drawer in her desk. She pulled out the two files that she had stored there. Then she turned around and left the office, locked the door and strode quickly back to the conference room.

She entered and went to her seat.

She opened the thin file and kept it next to the two photos.

"Chee Wee," she called, "please come here and tell me what you see."

Chee Wee stood next to Julia and bent over. He looked carefully at the two photos and the photo in the file.

He frowned and pointed.

"This is the same man," he said, "but how…"

Julia smiled in triumph.

"Yes, this is the man who came out of the restroom after Closier went in," she almost crowed. "Lee Sun Wah. He was found dead four days later in MacRitchie Reservoir."

Chee Wee looked stunned.

"That cannot be a coincidence!" he exclaimed.

"It is not a coincidence," said Julia, grimly.

Her peripheral vision had proved to be correct.

There was more to Greg Closier's death than initially assumed.

"I will need to take this to the Superintendent," she said.

While she glanced at her watch, she yawned. It was past 9:00 pm.

"It's late, let's pack up now, and deal with this on Monday."

Mr. Lee was not going anywhere over the weekend, anyway.

CHAPTER 15

Saturday morning found me on the tennis court doing my best to get rid of the insidious after-effects of previous night's Laksa and Chendol.

After three sets, of which Raymond and I lost two, I felt virtuous. Tired but virtuous.

"Thanks, guys," I said, as we were towelling off in the locker room.

"What a great game!" said Chow Pin.

"You are always in a good mood when you win," complained Raymond, good naturedly.

"What can I say, I am human," laughed Chow Pin.

"We will get you next time," threatened Raymond.

"Can't wait!" jeered Simon, as he went towards the showers.

I said my goodbyes and left.

Nysa had had to attend a lunch and needed the car. Her lunches started at 11:00 am and ended by around 5:00 pm.

I reached our condo by 9:30 am and took the elevator to our apartment.

After a muscle-rejuvenating shower, I joined her for

breakfast. She was not eating. She sat with me, sipping on a cup of tea.

"I know I promised you the next batch of Christmas cake, but it isn't ready yet," she apologised.

Thank God, I thought.

"Oh, what a pity," I said.

Complete honesty in relationships is overrated.

"So where is lunch today?" I asked.

"We are going to Bowring Farm," she said, "a new restaurant in Seletar. People say it's amazing. Fusion cuisine."

"Great, have fun," I said, "By the way, has Randall reverted?"

"Not yet," said Nysa, "but he will, don't worry. And if he doesn't, it's his loss. He knows the value I can add."

We cleared the dishes, and I went to the study.

There was nothing imminent today, except that I had to gently break the news to James Hong that he was not going to be seeing Serena today.

But I would do that a little later, around 2:00 pm.

For now, I needed to look for and find restaurants and bars that matched the specifications that were needed for a last supper.

I fired up my laptop and started my search.

At 10:30 am, Nysa came into the study.

"Darling, I am off," she said, "How do I look?"

She looked gorgeous, as always.

"Beautiful, my love," I said, sincerely, "you are going to cause heads to spin!"

She smiled her delightful smile, which lit up her eyes and most of Singapore.

"I have made lunch for you," she said, as she kissed me,

"Siti will serve you."

"Don't worry," I told her, "go and enjoy yourself."

After Nysa left, I continued shortlisting eateries and bars.

I did not consider any restaurants or bars in hotels. There were too many hoops to jump through – doormen, bell boys, front desk staff, concierges. Too many people who notice and are trained to remember.

I also rejected most of the fancier fine dining places. Same problem.

My focus was on the smaller independents in places like Clarke Quay, the riverside, Arab Street. Where the turnaround times were short, where wait staff and bus boys were busy, where nooks were dimly lit.

I read reviews, opened websites, took virtual tours, scanned photographs.

I knew some places. Others were new to me.

By lunchtime, I had a list of eleven possibilities, of which Nysa and I had been to four, and I had been to one more with a friend.

I shut down the laptop and went to have my lunch.

After a light meal of salad, dal curry and prata, during which I binged on two episodes of Big Bang Theory, I went back to my study and logged into Facebook as Serena Woo.

I had already mentally drafted my message to James.

Oh, James,

I am so sorry.

My grandmother fell down and hurt herself at lunchtime.

I rushed over here.

We need to take her to the doctor.

Please forgive me.

Will message you as soon as I can.
Multiple unintelligible emojis.

I used the appropriate syntax and sent it off to James.

I shut down the laptop. I was supposed to be at the doctor.

Then I went to the bedroom, lay down and took my Saturday afternoon siesta.

Or tried to.

My mind was too fired up for me to sleep.

There were so many moving parts.

For an obsessive planner like me, moving parts are anathema. I like pieces to fall into place and remain still.

Should I use poison? Or should I use something sharper?

Should I set the stage in a restaurant? Or a movie theatre? Or at James' apartment?

Should I create an alibi for myself?

What if the situation doesn't work? What if the plan falls apart?

Sorry, do I understand that you are feeling confused?

Look, I know that the assassins you have encountered in movies and serials are steely, unemotional, stoic, stone-cold professionals. I am aware that they don't fret like this. Action is their watchword. Success is their goal. And all that crap.

Please understand, I am not a professional. Yet.

I don't have a back-office support team that sends me messages on my Ray Bans. I don't have the ability to hack phones and find out that my victim is going to be driving a blue Bentley into the Golden Landmark parking lot at 2:23 pm.

No one has found it in themselves to give me a machine

that creates lifelike masks that will allow me to become 4 inches taller, grow a sixpack and impersonate a Russian oligarch.

I was just an ordinary person. I lacked expertise, I didn't have the tools, I spent 40 years selling stuff to morons, for God's sake!

I was trying to bring to bear everything that I had learned through my life and career to help me execute my assignment successfully.

But too many things were outside my control.

I got off the bed and walked to the living room and then to the balcony. If at all there was a time for a cigarette, this was it.

I lit one, not really seeing the golden blanket of sunshine across the cityscape. All I was seeing was tripping and dropping the vial I was carrying. And pouring the poison into James' glass and a waiter crying out, 'hey, what is that?' And sitting across James as his eyes turned up into his head, and only then noticing a camera in the far corner filming every moment.

As I continued smoking, I calmed down.

I recognised these jitters. I used to have them when I was younger, when I was going to propose or present a new idea to my team or to the management. When I knew that I did not know enough and was worried that I would be caught out.

As I grew older, and more in command of my domain, I worried less. By now, I knew what I knew, and knew what to do about what I didn't know. Experience lends assurance, you know.

Now, I am back where I was 30 years ago. In a new role, in an unfamiliar domain.

No wonder.

I finished the cigarette and stubbed it out.

I looked at the view spread out before me and took a deep breath.

All will be well, I told myself.

CHAPTER 16

Nysa returned at 4:45 pm, carrying with her spoils of her lunch.

"Ishmael!" she announced, when she saw me, "Randall confirmed!"

"Wow!' I exclaimed, "great news! When?"

"About an hour ago," Nysa replied, "he sent me a WhatsApp message and said he would follow it up with an e-mail."

"Congratulations, Nysa!" I said, so glad that our approach worked, "you are in the big leagues now!"

Nysa unpacked and laid out the food that she had spirited away. One of the dishes was a brilliant pandan garlic biryani. Very contrasting flavours, but somehow melding into a delicious aftertaste. Another was a Falafel curry, which was astonishingly good.

After I had tasted everything and expressed appropriate delight, Nysa went into the kitchen to fetch herself some tea.

I walked to the study to check what was happening on Facebook.

I logged in.

James had felt very let down, it seemed.

He had tried his best not to whine, but had failed.

He came across as a petulant child who had been refused a treat.

Oh, I was so looking forward to this.

I had spent so much time preparing.

I had made a reservation at Jamie's. I had to cancel the reservation at the last minute. The restaurant was not happy.

I had told my friends that I was busy and now I had nothing to do.

By the way, I hope your grandmother is okay.

Why, oh why, does this always happen to me?

If I had answered right away, I would have given James a piece of mind that was not Serena's.

I took a few minutes. I tried to sink into Serena's persona.

I responded that I was still at the doctor's with my grandmother.

Oh, sorry, dear James.

I, too, was really looking forward to this.

My grandmother, she is very stubborn. She lives alone and doesn't allow anyone to help.

This is the second time this year that she has fallen down.

I feel so bad.

I will surely make it up to you when we meet.

As I wrote, I wondered why people were so needy.

Why does self-worth seem to depend so much on others' perceptions and expectations?

Don't people understand that they are the best judges of themselves? That they need to know themselves, accept themselves and appreciate themselves? Rather than seeking validation from relatives, friends, colleagues and even strangers?

Even though I knew for a fact that Serena did not exist, I felt sad that she was programmed to a life of quiet misery, forever seeking confirmation, needing others' opinions to find relevance.

Ding.

James had responded.

He sounded a little mollified.

I am glad that you are there for your grandmother.

Family is very important.

I love my grandparents very much.

When do you think we can meet?

Unrelated group of emojis that don't make any sense.

I gave it a few minutes.

Then, Serena responded,

You are so sweet.

I will not be able to meet tomorrow also. My mother has asked me to stay with my grandmother.

She is very silly, but she is my family.

Can we meet next Friday? Or the weekend?

Oh, got to go now, doctor is calling.

Bye.

Emoji, emoji, emoji.

I logged out of Facebook. I didn't want to see anymore of James for now.

To calm myself, I dove into the internet and read about poisons and their creative uses till it almost was time for dinner.

Then, I shut the laptop, swivelled my chair and looked out at the darkening sky.

What can one do about the Serenas of this world? I wondered.

So often, girls are conditioned from childhood to seek to please and praise and prattle. They are taught to beautify their faces and bodies, but not to reinforce their minds and spirits.

Why do parents and schools not teach adaptability and resilience? Why are children, especially girls, not trained in developing self-assurance and inner strength?

Almost every lesson, formal or extra-curricular, is about external validation – grades and ranks and awards and prizes and prom dates and popularity.

I had seen this so many times through my career. I had counselled and mentored and guided and pushed.

Most of the time, it was too late. The clay had hardened and could not be re-moulded. The person was imprisoned in walls largely of their own making, though social norms and values contributed to the mortar that bound the stones in the wall.

I shook myself and stood up.

Accept what you cannot change, Ishmael.

I washed up and went to the living room seeking light.

I found Nysa.

She was on the phone, talking and laughing.

I opened the wine cooler and poured her a glass of Rosé and took it to her.

She accepted it, mouthed a 'thank you' and continued on her call.

I sat in the sofa opposite.

I watched Nysa, her animation as she spoke, her unfettered laugh, the way emotions played on her face.

Why was she different?

She didn't bother herself about what other people thought of her. She didn't strive to live up to any expectations but her own. She gave more than she got, she offered help without qualification, she contributed without quid pro quos.

What caused one to fly and the other to fear?

"Ishmael," said Nysa, interrupting my morose train of thought.

"Yes, dear," I said.

"I wanted to talk to you about two things," she said, "one, I have received Randall's e-mail and the revised agreement. I have gone through it and it seems fine. May I send it to you for a quick review? Just to make sure I haven't missed anything?"

"Of course," I said, "my pleasure. And once again, congratulations, Nysa, I am so happy for you."

"Thank you, sweetheart," said Nysa, "and the second thing - it's Shahed's thirty-fifth birthday next month," she said, excitement entering her voice, "Marianna is planning a surprise party!"

"Nysa," I said in a warning tone, sitting forward, "Most people don't like surprise parties. It would be best to tell him about the surprise party beforehand."

"Foo!" she exclaimed, dismissively, "you are such a stick in the mud. I am sure he will love the party. I know that I love surprises!"

"Nysa," I said, again, "you are annoyed when Siti uses gula melaka instead of brown sugar when making brittle. Trust me, you don't like surprises."

"You don't know me at all!" she said, standing up and preparing to flounce out of the room, "After so many years

of marriage!"
    As promised, she flounced.
    I sat back in the sofa, shaking my head.
    When am I ever going to learn?

CHAPTER 17

On Sundays, on most Sundays, Nysa and I take a morning walk together.

We find a new place which we haven't visited, or a place we visited some time ago, and delight ourselves in the ordinary.

This Sunday, we went to Seletar lake.

It was cloudy and cool. The lake reflected the grey in the sky and the calm in the air.

We parked the car and started walking clockwise around.

Nysa told me all about the plans for Shahed's party.

They were going to hire the Tourmaline Ball Room at the US Club.

There would be about 50 guests.

She was organizing a band.

There would be dancing.

With every new sentence, my heart sank.

I don't like parties.

They are unnecessary, noisy, showy, pretentious, painful, tiring and plain annoying.

Mostly, they are opportunities for one-upmanship.

I tried to find solace in the beauty around me, in the yellow butterflies that fluttered past, at the baby monitor lizard which scurried into the water when it heard us coming.

It didn't work.

My mood was gradually getting danker.

When Nysa paused, I said, "May I run for a few minutes and return?"

Without waiting for a response, I started jogging.

As the endorphins started flooding my body, everything faded – my worries over James Hong, my fretting over Serena's fate, my irritation with the party – I could only hear and feel the steady metronomic thump of my shoes on the pathway, and the puffs of breath as they left my mouth.

I ran for about a kilometre and turned back and ran toward Nysa.

As I saw her approaching, I slowed down, turned and fell in step with her.

The lake shone, the sky hovered, breeze bristled.

Running solves so many problems.

Or not.

Nysa had exhausted the party topic.

She had moved on to the choices of gifts.

"Should we get him a new car?" she asked, "his Prius is so boring, and I am his mother saying this!"

"Nysa, do you know how much a new car costs?" I asked.

"About two hundred thousand dollars?" she suggested.

"Yes, and I am not going to give a two hundred-thousand-dollar gift to anyone!" I said. "We are well off, but not crazy rich."

"Shahed's our only son," she said, "everything we have is his anyway."

We have had this discussion before.

"Yes, I agree," I said, "and he will have everything once we are memories. Till then, he will make do with the paltry five hundred thousand dollars that he and Marianna earn together."

Nysa had a strange relationship with money.

She would try and save two dollars by parking (illegally) by the kerb rather than in the car park next door. She would go all the way to Serangoon Road and Buffalo Road to buy vegetables because CS Fresh were 'robbers, they charge so much for everything!"

Then, she would spend a couple of thousand dollars on a whim and not feel the pain.

She reminded me so much of the adage, "a single death is a misfortune, a million deaths is a statistic."

Also, Shahed and Marianna were one-percenters. They did not need expensive gifts from retired parents.

Finally, Shahed drove a Prius because he was woke, not because he couldn't afford a more muscular car. He thought he was saving the environment. Why he didn't take a bus or the MRT, I had no idea.

"Okay, you win," said Nysa, "if not a car, then what? Should we buy them an apartment?"

I started running again.

This time I ran almost two kilometres.

Does my wife think I am Midas? Every time the stock market hiccups, I feel an aneurysm coming on. I am starkly aware that I don't have any runway left. Whatever we have earned and saved and invested is what we have.

Don't get me wrong. We are not eking out a living. We are well off. We have more money than we need. But, nowadays, death is uncertain. People are increasingly living to their nineties. Inflation is certain. Prices have gone up by 6% this year alone. In this scenario, splurging money on expensive gifts is best done by children for their parents. After all, they have a steadily replenishing income stream, unlike ours in which source has dried.

As I turned around, an idea shouldered past the endorphins and struck me.

So far, I have been a pro bono assassin.

Is it possible to develop a revenue stream from this new vocation?

The thought intrigued me.

How would one go about hiring out one's services?

Where would one find clients?

What would be the right pricing strategy?

As I pondered alternate approaches and options, I neared Nysa, slowed down and joined her in walking again.

"Why are you running off every time I start discussing something important?" she asked querulously.

"How are parties and over-the-top gifts important?" I asked.

Nysa put on her 'puss in boots' look.

"Shahed and Marianna just went through a horrible episode," she said, her large eyes looking doleful, "all I want to do is make them happy again."

"Great," I said, "make them your olive and garlic fried rice and the lemon parfait. If that doesn't make them happy, nothing will."

She slapped me hard on my upper arm.

"You have no feelings!" Nysa cried, "you are a robot!"

"Ow, that hurt," I said.

"Good, you deserve it."

We walked in silence.

After a few steps, Nysa spoke again.

"What about a round-the-world trip?" she asked. "They haven't taken a break for quite a while."

I took a deep breath.

"Nysa, my dearest," I said, in my best mansplaining voice, "Shahed and Marianna are adults. They are quite well off. If they want a car or an apartment or a vacation, they can afford to have it. They could choose to have all three if they so wish. They don't need us to subsidise them."

"But I want to do something special," she whined.

"Fried rice, murtabak, coconut stew and lemon parfait," I suggested, "that is more special than anything else."

Nysa threw me a look. If she could have. she would have thrown me into the lake.

When we reached the car, Nysa turned to me.

"If you don't like any of my ideas," she said in an annoyed tone, "what do you have in mind for Shahed's birthday?"

I am going to give him a Joint Managing Partner, I thought.

And, boy, is that going to be some surprise!

"I will think of something," I said.

"Ha!" Nysa retorted as she got in and buckled her seat belt.

Just wait and see, my dear.

INTERLUDE 5

As Ishmael Dollah argued with Nysa on the merits of different gifts for Shahed,

Inspector Julia Binti Shafiq vacuumed her living room.

Sunday was her day for chores. Yippee!

After vacuuming, she would have to mop the kitchen, wash the bathroom and the wash closet, move the laundry over to the dryer, and clean out the freezer.

I should never have let Rosalyn go, she thought, as she pulled the 8 kg monster around. I could have been lounging in bed. Or watching TV. Or both.

Her foot caught on the spooling wire, and she stumbled, but caught herself before face planting.

Gggghh, she growled and yanked the errant wire to teach it a lesson.

Julia neared the TV console. As she pushed the floor brush underneath, she felt it hit something. Keeping the tube aside, she got onto her hands and knees to see what was underneath.

It was a photo frame.

As she pulled it out, she knew that she shouldn't, that she

should leave it where it was. But inertia took over, and she raised it and turned it over.

It was a photo from her wedding.

She and Aman, looking unbelievable young and radiantly happy.

Promptly, her eyes misted over.

She wiped the glass with her hand, trying to remove the layer of dust.

The vacuum cleaner motor was still humming. She leaned over and hit the button, and it wound down petulantly.

She sat on her ankles and calves and looked at the photo.

How much in love we were, she thought. How happy we felt. The world was not big enough for our dreams.

Aman and she were classmates from grade 5. He was the quiet, studious, ignored one and she was the tomboy, aggressive, athletic and popular. She did not notice him till grade 8, when she was struggling with a concept in physics and needed help.

"Ask Aman, he's the class genius" she was told.

So, she did. She walked up to him that afternoon and tapped him on his shoulder.

"Hey Aman," she said.

He looked up. His face showed surprise, even a hint of shock.

"Yes," he asked, in his soft voice.

"I need some help with understanding Newton's laws of motion," she said, "can you help me?"

"Of course," he replied. "Do you want to start now?"

She found him kind, patient, helpful and persistent. He never gave up, even if he had to explain something ten times.

Within a week, she had fallen in like with him.

Within a month she had decided that she had found the man she would marry.

Julia wiped her eyes on her sleeves.

She kept the photo frame face down on the console.

She stood up, picked up the hose, started the vacuum cleaner and continued towards the dining table.

CHAPTER 18

Nysa drove us back to our condo.

As we drove, I was thinking about the idea that had struck me while running.

Could assassination be a vocation rather than a mere pastime?

Would the risk-reward equation be worthwhile?

How much would an assassination fetch? How many could one do safely each year? Did it need to be a local operation, or could it expand to a regional, even global one?

What was the market size? Was there a defined target client demographic?

It would be interesting to draft a business case, I thought. At least I would know what the gaps are, and whether there was any way to fill them.

I felt a sense of anticipation, much like I did in the past when we had to establish a presence in a new geography or market segment.

Always start with 'why', I told myself.

Why should I make assassination my business?

One, there was a clear market need. I was sure that there

were many, many clients wanting people removed from their lives and willing to reward the forwarding agents.

Two, I believe my skill set suits the general requirements. Yes, I am old, but I am also organised, patient and persistent. I have time, I don't panic. I know how to adapt to changing circumstances quickly and effectively. Yes, there is a lot to learn, but I am also a quick learner.

Three, the barriers of entry to this market were quite high. Most people don't have the ability, willingness or temperament to be an assassin. So, competition was likely to be meagre.

Four, I suspect that the profit margins would be quite high. Much higher than a consultancy or as an executive coach. Question to be answered - would the fee be inclusive or exclusive of costs?

"Ishmael, we have reached," said Nysa.

I looked out of the windshield. Yes, we were in our basement car park.

I turned to look at Nysa.

"What were you thinking of? A special gift for Shahed?" she asked, "You looked like you were planning something, all excited like a child with a new toy."

"Something like that," I replied with a smile.

We got out and walked to the elevator.

"By the way," I said, as I remembered, "I have been invited for drinks today. You remember Derek Francis? My Australian friend?"

"Yes, Shu Ling's husband," she said, immediately. Nysa remembers everyone, even if she has met them in passing. "Where are you meeting?

"At the Island Club," I said, "around 6:30 pm."

"Will you be back for dinner?" she asked, as the elevator reached our floor.

"I am not sure, Nysa," I replied, "Don't wait up. One thing I learnt working with Aussies is that once they start drinking, they don't stop till the bar closes."

She laughed.

"Come, let's have breakfast, I am starving," she said, as we entered our apartment.

After a shower and breakfast, I returned to the study.

I opened the laptop and logged first into Serena Woo's Facebook account.

I spent about 30 minutes telling the world about my grandmother and her obstinacy, and then about how I loved her very much and how sweet she was. And, in the process, how dutiful and caring I was. I had to ensure that Serena's persona and the illusion around her persona was maintained and developed continuously.

Then, I responded to James Hong's two messages.

He had asked about her grandmother in one and indicated his eagerness to meet on the coming Friday in the other. I told him that I was still looking after her and unless something drastic happened, I would surely meet him on Friday.

I cooed and breathed heavily into his feed, complimenting him on a couple of his posts, to stroke his ego and signed off.

I then checked my email.

There was an e-mail from Aziz:

Hi, Chief,

Item received.

Putting it into my shipment, which will leave tomorrow morning.

Should be in Singapore by Tuesday.

Do you want me to arrange to deliver it to your place, or will you pick it up from our company stockist at Ubi?

I have also included the material data sheet in the package. Take care when you handle it, seems quite dicey.

Cheers…

That was great! The week was starting well. Or ending well, depending on which school of thought you belonged to.

I replied immediately.

Hey, Aziz,

Thank you, that was quick!

I will pick the package up from your stockist, no worries. Please send me the address and the contact person.

Thanks for the data sheet. I am arranging to use this in a sterilised lab, so we are good.

Shall update you once I have it.

I owe you one!

Take care, all the best…

I opened my calendar and checked the plan for Tuesday.

This was a reflex from my past. Nowadays, most of my calendar was a sea of white blankness.

Tuesday, predictably, was wide open.

"Pick up package", I wrote in the 12:00 noon slot.

Moving on from Outlook, I opened the file where I had stored the names of the outlets that sold ice picks and spikes. They were scattered across Singapore, but one of them, "A to Z Novelties" was in Ubi. Yes, I would combine this with my Tuesday trip.

I closed my laptop. Enough work, today was Sabbath.

I picked up my iPad, sat on the settee in the study and

opened the latest issue of The Economist. The cover bemoaned the state of British politics. I started to read.

After about an hour and a half, in which time I had lost all hope for the world and its future, Nysa called me for lunch. I shut the iPad with a sense of relief and went to the dining room.

Lunch was a corn salad, lentil and yogurt soup, and Christmas cake.

The salad was crisp and crunchy, the soup was amazingly flavourful, but the Christmas cake took the cake and ate it too. Wow! I took three pieces, knowing that I would be running almost to Changi tomorrow, but it was worth it.

After that it was straight to the bedroom for our siesta. I tried to read a little more of The Economist but dropped off before the first paragraph ended.

Waking at around 5:00 pm, I went and made tea for Nysa and brought it to her in bed.

"Thank you, sweetie," she said, sleepily.

"I am going to shower, change and leave by 6:00 pm," I said, "don't wait up, sweetheart."

"Okay, see you," she responded, and burrowed deeper into the covers.

The drive to the Island Club was slow. There was more traffic than I expected on a Sunday evening.

I reached at 6:25 pm, parked and walked to the Island Bar, which was Derek's second home.

It was a beautiful room, large but somehow intimate, overlooking the lush greenery.

"Ishmael, here!" Derek called from the corner on the right.

I steered to the small sofa suite he occupied. He rose and

gave me a hug, which I returned. I liked him. I sat in the sofa next to him, at a right angle.

Derek called the waiter and ordered a dark rum and coke for me without asking me. He also ordered another beer for himself.

The drinks came very quickly. We toasted our friendship and our respective wives.

After about five minutes, Derek leaned forward.

"Ishmael," he said, his normally jovial tone quite subdued, "I wanted to catch up because I have a problem that I have been struggling with. I need some advice."

I leaned forward too and kept my glass on the table.

"Of course, Derek," I said, "how can I be of help?"

"I need to find a way to get rid of one of my senior managers," he said, "and I heard that you are the best person to guide me."

CHAPTER 19

My heart stopped for a moment.

How the hell did Derek know? How much did Derek know?

I tried to keep my emotions off my face. I leaned over and picked up my glass.

"Mm-hmm," I said.

"Did you know that many of our friends call you 'Hitman' behind your back?" he asked, not noticing my rigidity.

"Mm-hmm," I said, taking a sip of my drink.

"Yes," he continued, "everyone talks about how you ruthlessly decimated the management teams in your last two companies. And how you did this without a single lawsuit or complaint to the Ministry of Manpower!"

I let out the breath that I hadn't known I was holding.

"I wouldn't use the word 'ruthlessly'," I said mildly.

Derek laughed.

"You may not," he said, "but others surely do!"

"I hear that you got rid of the entire C-Suite in Borgian Holdings," he continued, "and that, too, within a week,"

I took another sip.

"Well," I said, "they had run the company to the ground

while pulling high 6-figure salaries. What was I supposed to do? Rap them on their knuckles?"

"No, Ishmael," he protested, "don't misunderstand me. We think you are a rockstar! You turned around two companies that most of us wouldn't have touched with a barge pole. The one thing I don't understand is why you hung up your boots so young? You have many years left in you, my friend."

"Ruthlessness leaves one tired and depleted," I said, wryly.

He roared with laughter.

"I have seen you playing tennis at the Club," he said when he stopped, "and neither of these adjectives even remotely applies to you."

"Why don't you tell me about your problem," I suggested, "and we can look at approaches to solving it."

Derek took a huge swig of his beer. He adjusted himself on his sofa.

"Okay, here goes," he said, visibly girding himself.

Derek Francis was the CEO of Jetsmart, a regional industrial conglomerate headquartered in Singapore. The group dealt with diverse lines of business relating to mining, transportation, trading and warehousing. He had been the CEO for more than a decade, as far as I remembered.

He was, in addition to being knowledgeable and capable, an amazing people person. He owned every room he was in. His network numbered in the thousands. He was a genuinely nice person, caring and helpful.

I had helped Derek a couple of times in the past. He has always gone the extra mile whenever I have needed. If I could help Derek with his current situation, I surely would.

"The Group Vice President of Sales is a guy named Rahul Sinha," he started. "He has been with the Group for about 5-6 years. He is about thirty-six years old. Quite smart, knows his stuff, achieves his targets."

"Mm-hmm," I prompted.

"As you know, Ishmael, some people who do well start believing that they are gods. And that they are owed more than what they are getting."

"Yes, I have come across the type," I murmured.

"Well, Rahul is the epitome of the type," said Derek, after taking another gulp of beer. "Over the past couple of years, he has started believing that he is invincible. He has become increasingly toxic in his behaviour with his colleagues and subordinates. He bullies and threatens and browbeats."

"Mm-hmm,"

"He is not a fool," cautioned Derek, "so far, he has been behaving well with his superiors. All sweetness and light. But even that is gradually shifting. About two weeks ago, when the CFO asked for some explanations on his division's monthly costs, it seems he was 'arrogant and dismissive' as Helen reported to me later."

"I have met Helen," I said, "I would tend to believe what she says."

"Yes, I do," he agreed, "she did not want to make a mountain of this. She just wanted to keep me apprised of the situation."

"Smart lady," I nodded, "well grounded."

"Rahul also has the Board eating out of his hand," continued Derek, coming to the crux of the matter. "It doesn't hurt that he is the nephew of the majority shareholder, Mr. Jindal, his mother's brother."

"Aah," I said, "that puts a new complexion to the situation."

"To be fair, so far, Rahul has never exploited that relationship," said Derek, "but something seems to have changed over the past few months. He is more aggressive, more assured. Almost as if he knows something that I do not."

"And you cannot ask him to leave," I stated matter-of-factly.

Derek groaned.

"That's the effing problem," he said, as he waved to attract the attention of the waiter. "He delivers solid outcomes. He is connected. He is related to Mr. Jindal. I will need substantial justification to do anything."

He paused. The waiter came to the table and Derek ordered another beer. He looked at me. I showed him my almost full glass.

"There is a little more than what you have said so far, isn't there, Derek?" I suggested.

Derek looked at me sharply for a few seconds. Then he laughed aloud.

"You are one shrewd bastard, aren't you, Ishmael?" he chuckled, "very little escapes you."

"And?" I asked.

He took a deep breath.

"I think Rahul is after my job," he said. "I don't have any evidence of this, but you and I, we have been around the block. We know how to read signs."

I definitely don't know how to read signs, but I let it pass.

"Mm-hmm," I said.

"I am worried that, as the Group's main rainmaker, he will be taken seriously if he throws his hat in the ring," said Derek, looking anxiously towards the bar for his beer.

I understood. It was not about Rahul as much as it was about Derek.

A CEO has many responsibilities ranging from acquiring customers, increasing revenue, maintaining profit margins, holding on to people, satisfying regulators, sucking up to the Board.

But, in the corporate world, a CEO's primary responsibility is to remain CEO.

To hold on for as long as possible. Even if they are well past their sell-by date.

To do this, they will move mountains.

They will fudge accounts, report unreal figures, step on any number of backs, kowtow to the powers-that-be.

It is almost as if the position is an integral part of their identity.

The waiter came and placed another stein of beer in front of Derek, who leapt at it.

"What do you think I can do to help, Derek?" I asked, as he glugged a quarter down.

"Tell me what I can and should do?" he said, tentatively. "Have you faced such a situation before? If yes, how did you deal with it?"

"Derek, may I be blunt?" I asked.

"Ishmael, when are you not?" he shot back. "Go on, hold nothing back."

"Are you really worried about Rahul's negative impact on the Group, or is this about your future?" I asked, looking him in the eye.

"You don't pull your punches, do you?" he said as his face turned reddish with emotion.

"Sorry," I said, smiling, "I have found that beating around the bush is not worth a bird in the hand."

He laughed.

"Give me a minute," he said. He took another deep swig, his gaze turning inward. And another. Then he turned to me.

"I won't lie, Ishmael," he said. "I want to continue as CEO. No question. But I am seriously worried about what Rahul can do to the Group. I have spent almost fifteen years with Jetsmart. We have built an amazing team, a fantastic business. But, as you know, all this is fragile. One or two bad years, and we can be facing bankruptcy. I don't want to see that happen. And I am afraid that it will, if Rahul is allowed his way."

"Also," he continued, "even if he doesn't become CEO, he is gradually disrupting the team and the workplace. He is hurting Jetsmart. He needs to go,"

"Thank you," I said, "I understand and appreciate your being honest."

I took a sip from my drink.

"May I take a couple of days to think about whatever you said?" I asked.

"Of course," said Derek.

"Also, regarding Rahul, do you have any information…" I started.

"I knew it!" said Derek triumphantly, as he held up a buff envelope. "'If you go to Ishmael, go prepared', everyone said. 'He will ask you for a file', they said. Well, here you are!"

I laughed.

"I didn't know that I was so predictable," I said, as I took the envelope from his hand.

CHAPTER 20

About fifteen years ago, I picked up a book called, "The Secret".

This was one of those self-help books that come out every few years that become a cultish hit and sell millions of copies. (I picked up someone else's copy)

The simplistic premise of "The Secret" is the "law of attraction."

Essentially, the author insists, whatever you think about is what you will eventually get in life. So, if you think of things you don't want, you will only get the things you don't want. However, if you only focus on the things you want, then you will get everything you want in life.

The author even claims that the Secret works because the Universe is made up of energy and all energy has a frequency. She posits that your thoughts also emit a frequency, and therefore, the frequency of your thoughts will resonate with the frequency of the Universe's energy.

I didn't finish the book.

It was utter bullshit.

As the years passed, I evolved my own premise.

It is not a secret. It is not even mine. It is an extrapolation of an old psychological concept called 'confirmation bias'.

This premise, called the 'law of awareness' consists of just three points –

Point one: just as Google is bursting with information, the Universe is awash with opportunities.

Point two: if I don't have a smart phone or a computer, or if I don't have the desire for information, I would not open and browse Google. So, all that information is there, but I don't access it, and thus, it is lost to me. However, if I have the means and the motive, the world's knowledge is available to me, and I can choose to learn about anything I care to.

Point three: the Universe works much the same. If I don't have the ability or the desire to look for opportunities, I will never find them, and thus, they are lost to me. If I have the means and motive, all the Universe's opportunities are accessible, and I can choose which ones I want to explore.

That's it. It doesn't need a book.

I often share a simple example with my mentees.

Imagine that you are driving on a two-lane road for one hundred kilometres. You can see the cars on both sides of the road.

For the first fifty kilometres, you are looking out of the window, but with no specific motive.

At the end of this first half of the drive, I ask you how many white Toyota Corollas you have noticed.

You will look blankly at me and say, none.

Now, your mind is made aware by my question.

For the next fifty kilometres, whether you want to or not, you are primed to look for white Toyota Corollas.

And, mindbogglingly, you will see dozens of them.

You passed a similar number of white Corollas in both halves of the journey. In the first half, you did not seek them, so you did not find them. In the second half, by virtue of being made aware, you sought them (even involuntarily), and you found more than you ever thought you would.

The lesson from my premise is – keep yourself open to opportunities, and you will come across more of them. Seek, and you shall find.

Why am I telling you all this?

Derek and I finished our drinks (five of his and one of mine) and crossed over to The Lookout, a lovely restaurant that I have eaten at before. They have a wide selection of cuisines.

Derek went Western and I went Asian.

With tacit agreement, we moved on from the topic of Rahul Sinha. He spoke about the latest big initiative in Jetsmart, digitalizing the entire supply chain, and how it was changing the speed at which business happened.

We spoke about his children, both of whom were in Australia, and about Marianna and Shahed.

I left at about 10:00 pm.

As I drove back home, I was thinking about the law of attraction and the law of awareness.

Just this morning, I was thinking about assassination as a business opportunity.

And now, Derek needs a troublesome employee terminated.

Did the Universe's energy resonate with that of my thoughts?

Or is Rahul Sinha an opportunity that I wouldn't have

noticed if I had not thought about monetising assassination?

Can you make something happen my just thinking about it?

Or does thinking about something open doors that were previously flush with the walls around you?

As I arrived at our condo, I recalled the immortal words from 'Hamlet',

"There are more things in Heaven and Earth, Horatio, than are dreamt of in your philosophy."

I found Nysa in the living room, working on her latest research project on Tipu Sultan, an amazingly brave King of Mysore in the eighteenth century, who was also an inventor and political and social innovator.

"Hi, sweetheart," I said, as I entered.

She looked up and smiled.

"Had a good evening?" she asked, "How are Derek and Shu Ling?"

"Everyone is good," I replied, "and yes, I had a nice evening. Derek is having some problems in his company which he needed some advice on."

I filled her in briefly on Derek's concerns. I kept Rahul Sinha's name out of the discussion.

"Poor Derek," said Nysa, "this stupid fellow must be such a thorn in his side."

"That he surely is," I agreed.

"You go ahead to bed, I will join you in half hour or so," said Nysa, "I need to finish this section tonight."

"No worries," I said, "I need to do some reading, too. See you soon."

I went down to the study. I changed, had a quick wash, and sat down on the couch.

I opened the envelope that Derek had given me and extracted the slim grey file. It contained only about twenty-five pages or so.

I opened it and started reading.

It started with Rahul's resume. Then his performance evaluations over the past three years. His remuneration package and its trend over the past three years.

So far, all the documents pointed to a capable employee who was achieving, even surpassing, whatever he had promised.

The last ten pages were copies of complaints received by HR.

These pointed to an employee who had allowed success to go to his head, to his worst instincts coming out and creating disharmony and disruption around him.

Then, there was a note from the Vice President of HR to Derek. This listed the number of resignations that had taken place over the last 3 months, with the proximate cause being Rahul Sinha.

Seven people had left the company because they could not tolerate his behaviour anymore.

Four of the seven had spent more than a decade in Jetsmart; the others had spent at least five years each. What was even more dismaying was that three of the seven were deemed 'critical employees', who would take six months or more to replace.

I kept the file down on my lap.

This was a serious problem for Derek.

If he acted against Rahul, it could backfire due to Rahul's relationship with the Board and his uncle. If he did not take action, even more critical employees would depart, weakening the Group, impacting performance and outcome, and consequently, by hurting Derek's reputation and perception as a capable CEO.

I could see why he was worried.

I would need some time to parse the situation and seek possible approaches to resolving it.

But my instinct said that a traditional solution was unlikely. Just terminating Rahul's employment, even if that were possible, would be only a temporary fix. With his in on the Board, he would be back, even possibly as a Director, which was worse by an order of magnitude.

We would need to think outside the box.

And find a permanent solution.

INTERLUDE 6

As Ishmael Dollah read Rahul Sinha's file and pondered a permanent solution to Derek's problem,

Inspector Julia Binti Shafiq lay in bed, eyes open, staring at the ceiling fan's blades whirling above her.

She was exhausted but could not sleep.

Who was Lee Sun Wah?

Why was he in the Club?

Had he seen anything?

Had he actually died of natural causes, or did the coroner miss something, believing that a man in his seventies just sat on a park bench and passed on?

There wasn't even a possibility of exhuming the body; the family had claimed it and cremated it in accordance with their traditions.

Who was the other man who went into the restroom? Sadly, even the enhanced photos were not clear enough to seek a match with Club member records.

I need to check other camera feeds to see if Lee met anyone around that period, she thought.

She wanted to make a note but felt too tired to get up.

She turned on her side.

What happened with Aman and me?

Julia and Aman became inseparable in the eighth grade. They sat together, ate together, played together.

To everyone, they were the best of friends.

To Julia, she was with the boy who would become the man she would marry. He just didn't know it yet.

They changed each other.

Julia studied more. Her parents, who had almost given up, were shocked when her report card showed more Bs than Ds.

Aman played more. Julia taught him badminton and football. He could never beat her, but steadily improved to the point that she had to play at her best to beat him.

Julia started wearing dresses. Once in a while. Her mother was overjoyed. They went shopping together, and Julia even tried on eye liner.

Aman became more assertive. He was always the smartest person in class; now he started stating his opinions firmly and clearly.

They moved together to the ninth and then the tenth grades.

Their classmates wondered how two such dissimilar teenagers stayed such close friends.

One Saturday in the tenth grade, Julia, Aman and four of their friends went to a movie.

Julia and Aman sat together, naturally.

When the Velociraptor jumped out of the bush, Julia was startled. She reached for Aman's hand. He clasped her hand gently.

They continued holding hands through the movie. It was such a magical time, thought Julia sadly. What happened?

CHAPTER 21

Monday morning.

I was running by the river heading towards Marina Bay.

The sun was just making its presence felt.

The riverwalk was gorgeous, lined with trees and benches, curving first left and then right, flanked by renovated shop houses.

I was blind to the beauty. I kept seeing the complaints against Rahul Sinha in my mind.

"He berated me in front of the whole room, making me feel useless. I could not face my colleagues."

That was nasty and unnecessary. Any dressing down would have been as effective in private.

"He called me a lazy bitch and asked me why I even bothered to come to work,"

Deliberately hurtful, targeting the person rather than any issue or task.

"He is the worst boss I have ever had. He takes credit for all our work and passes on blame. He is never appreciative, never recognises our efforts."

A common complaint about bosses across the world.

Does such a person deserve redemption? Can such a person be redeemed at all?

Over the years I have learn that attitude is not something that can be changed easily. It is part of a person's DNA, a person's belief system. It becomes part of their identity.

What then are the possible conventional solutions to a problem like Rahul?

One, get him fired. That may fix the problem, temporarily, in Jetsmart. Rahul would find a similar role elsewhere. He would cause harm in his new workplace. He would hurt and alienate and disrupt.

Two, get him help. Find a way for Rahul to accept counselling and change his behaviour. Possible but not probable. People like Rahul don't know they have a problem. They refuse to accept that they are a problem. It is always 'others'. Never themselves.

And the unconventional one?

Three, get him out of the way. This would fix the problem permanently. But is it too draconian?

I reached Marina Barrage and continued running across it.

Crime and punishment are such fluid concepts, I thought.

If you murder a person, you can be executed or jailed for life.

If you hound or abuse a person until they consider their life not worth living, the law can do nothing to you.

Physical harm reaps immediate punishment. Mental abuse is not even in the law books.

I stopped at the East Bay and panted.

If Rahul Sinha was the reason for seven colleagues to leave the company, where they had spent many years working and earning their livelihood, isn't he responsible for the damage he has caused those seven lives?

I looked out at the sea.

It didn't have any answers.

I started running back, tired but none the wiser.

I may need to speak to Derek once again, I thought. I need a little more colour on the people who have left. What is the true impact on them – financially, emotionally, career-wise?

Nysa met me at the door of our apartment with a smoothie that looked like something had died a violent death in the mug.

"Here, Ishmael, try this," she said, "you will love it!"

I was too tired to resist.

I closed my eyes and emptied the mug in one go. It was surprisingly tasty.

"Wow," I said, "that was great, thanks!"

We walked in together as she told me about the ingredients in the smoothie. I hadn't ever heard of half the items she mentioned.

"So, what are you doing today?" she asked.

"I may step out once in the morning and again in the evening, I have a couple of tasks to complete," I said,

"I may have to go for a meeting with Epigram," she said. Epigram were local publishers who contracted Nysa regularly for their stable of authors. "it is not confirmed yet, I should know shortly. Is it okay if I take the car?"

"Of course, Nysa," I said, "It's all yours."

I left her in the living room and went for my shower. Feeling rehydrated and refreshed, I went into the study and opened the laptop.

The first order of the day was to check Serena's Facebook activity.

Thirty minutes later, the world knew more about Serena's grandmother than they ever wanted to or needed to know. James learnt that Serena would love to meet him on Friday evening, after work. She would suggest a place close to her office shortly. Serena added three new friends and re-posted a reel of a kitten climbing down a fence.

That done, I cursorily checked my email for any messages.

Someone from the Singapore Customs insisted that I click on the attached link and update my particulars.

There was an e-mail from Aziz with an address, a name and a phone number.

Any time after 12:00 noon, Chief.

I logged out and shut the laptop.

As I had told Nysa, I had two tasks to complete today

—

One, finalise the venue of Serena's meet with James. By finalise, I meant that I had to visit it, vet it and okay it.

I went into the appropriate folder and opened the list of eleven short-listed locations.

I would do the top five on my list today, the ones I had already visited at least once before. Three of them were around Arab Street and two on Lower Circular Road.

All of them were within three kilometres from our condo, so a pleasant walk away. I would do this between 6:30 and 8:00 pm, which would be around the time that Serena and James would meet.

Two, check out the other two shops selling ice picks and other sharp objects.

Both these places were in Ang Mo Kio, which meant that I needed a ride. Best to go by street hailed taxi paying cash or by bus using a pre-paid EZ Link card, I thought.

I opened the drawer and took out my alternate iPhone 14. This had a pre-paid SIM, not directly traceable to me. I keyed in the phone numbers of both shops.

"Nysa, I am stepping out to buy cigarettes," I called.

"Okay, see you," she called back.

I took the stairs down to the lobby and walked out of the condo to the petrol station about 500 metres away.

Just before I reached, I stopped under a bus stop awning.

I called both numbers and confirmed that they were open and that they had the items in stock.

They were and they had.

I stepped into the petrol station 7-11 store and purchased a pack of cigarettes. I had decided long ago that there was no point lying when the truth served as well.

I walked back to our condo and elevatored to the apartment, walking directly to the balcony to taste my new acquisition.

After savouring the last puff of the cigarette, I reluctantly stubbed it out. I pondered for a moment if I should light another.

No.

Miles to go before I smoke.

I went to Nysa's study. She was at her desk with books and papers scattered across it.

"So sorry to disturb, sweetheart," I said.

She looked at me and smiled.

"I have to step out for an hour and half or so," I said, "will be back for lunch. Any news from Epigram?"

"No, not yet, the meeting will only happen in the late afternoon or tomorrow," she replied.

"Okay, see you soon," I waved and left her to complete her study of the Maharajah of Mysore.

I changed into as nondescript clothes as possible – unbranded jeans, dark grey full-sleeved t-shirt with no logo, a black baseball cap, my specs which I rarely use and a Covid mask which I even more rarely use.

Once ready, I quickly tiptoed out. I did not want Nysa spotting me and telling me to change into something more presentable. My objective was to be absentable.

I left the apartment and got into the elevator, hoping that I would be able to come back with the tools I needed.

CHAPTER 22

I reached the first shop, Sim & Co, within half an hour. I was lucky to get a direct bus the very moment I reached the bus stop.

It was on the first floor of an HDB complex, along with a score of other outlets offering food, massages, beauty, baked goods, coffee and pet care. The Housing & Development Board is Singapore's public housing authority. HDB complexes are large, sprawling housing estates that combine apartments, commercial outlets and recreational facilities. They abound across Singapore.

I already had my cap, specs and mask on.

I opened the door and entered the store. As with such stores, it was chock a block with products piled everywhere. I threaded my way to the counter, which was halfway down the store.

"Hallo?" I called, "Good morning…"

The store door dinged open again.

Oh hell. I had hoped not to have company.

"Yes, what you want?" said the man who entered.

"Good morning, is this your shop?" I asked.

"Yes, what you want?" he asked again.

"I am looking for a marlin spike," I said, "do you have one?"

"Ah, yes, come," he instructed, and disappeared behind a pile.

I quickly followed.

Just a few metres away was a large bin. The man dipped into it and pulled out a plastic wrapped item.

"Like this?" he asked.

I took it from him.

It was a marlin spike, thin and deadly, about 9" long excluding the handle. It looked like it was made of stainless steel. If I were an author, I would have written about its evil glint.

"Nice," I said, noncommittally, "any others?"

The man leaned into the bin and pulled out another package.

"This one more expensive," he said, as he handed it over.

Another marlin spike, very similar to the first one, but in blued steel. This had a matte finish, and so did not have a glint, evil or otherwise.

"How much, sir?" I asked, politely.

"First one twenty-nine dollars, other one thirty-five dollars," he replied.

I would have liked to take the blued steel one, but the fastest way to leave an impression in a Singapore shop is to buy the more expensive of two items. It is absolutely not done. Such an act will be remembered; and tales would be told by campfires for many generations.

"That one," I said, pointing at the stainless-steel spike.

He turned and led me to the counter.

"Nets or Pay Wave?" he asked.

I made a pretence of searching my back pockets.

"Oh, forgot my wallet, so sorry," I said, looking all confused and lost. The man's face fell, and he started turning away.

Then I reached into my front pocket, searched, and pulled out a few notes. "Ah, no problem, I have cash."

"Good, good," said the storekeeper. "I give discount, only twenty-seven dollars."

"Oh, thank you so much," I said. I counted out the exact amount and passed it to him. He pulled a plastic bag from a hook, put the spike into it, and handed it over to me.

"Have a nice day," I said, as I manoeuvred my way to the door.

He waved his hand and grunted.

As soon as I exited, I wanted to open the packing and feel the marlin spike. I restrained myself. It would be unseemly to be caught on candid camera admiring a possible murder weapon. It would also be difficult to explain to the authorities.

Should I go to the other store, too? I wondered. I had the time.

The store was just two lanes away. I started walking briskly and reached "Jit Sun Hardware" in a few minutes. This store was in a sort of strip mall, sandwiched between a café and a pastry shop. It looked and seemed more organised than the previous one.

As I neared, I noticed through the glass window that the shop had at least three customers browsing.

I continued walking past the mall and reached the next bus stop. I had to wait for only four minutes before I was whisked away by a snazzy new double-decker bus that promised it was greening the nation.

I was home well before lunch time. I went to the study, shut the door and opened the package and took out the marlin spike. It looked even better when it was out of the plastic packaging. It was not very heavy, but solid. In a battle between flesh and spike, the latter would win effortlessly.

I put the spike in the plastic and tucked it away safely.

All this arms-dealing had whipped up an appetite. I walked to the dining room.

Nysa and Siti were just laying the table. I joined them in carrying the dishes from the kitchen to the table and put out the place mats and plates.

Nysa had made her signature Nasi Lemak, which she knew I loved. Accompanying it was a spicy chilly sambal.

The table was silent for a few minutes, other than the clink of cutlery on crockery. Only when I had inhaled half the bowl did I come up for air.

"This is amazing, Nysa," I said, taking a huge gulp of my Bandung, "Michelin star worthy!"

"Thank you, Ishmael," she said, "this is all Siti's doing."

"Thank you, Siti!" I called out to the kitchen, "Fantastic food!"

She came bustling out, wiping her hands on a towel.

"Thank you, sir," she simpered.

After finishing lunch and clearing the table, Nysa excused herself to continue work on her current project.

I went to the study, closed the door, and took out the marlin spike. I caressed it for a while and then spent some time getting used to holding it in different positions.

If we were sitting side by side, how should I hold it?

Underhand?

If I were standing beside him? In front of him? Behind him?

It was fun.

Then, I took out a pair of nitrile gloves which I had bought in my previous book. You would have known this if you had taken the trouble to read it.

I wore them and tried the various positions to ensure that the spike did not slip or move. It didn't.

Next, I went to the kitchen and rooted in the refrigerator for some fruit. I found half a watermelon and two apples. I brought them to the study on a tray.

I spent the next half hour killing the fruit in different ways. Yes, I knew they were innocent and did not deserve to be executed, but life was not always fair.

The watermelon was easier to kill. Once the initial resistance of the rind was overcome, it succumbed immediately. The apples put up little more of a fight. They were lighter and were difficult to pin down. Pun intended.

Once the slaughter had ceased, I ate the apples. That was the best way of getting rid of the evidence. Then, I took the mauled watermelon to the kitchen, confirmed that Siti was taking her afternoon nap, and cut it into slices, discarding those slices that showed signs of distress into the rubbish chute. I collected the slices into a bowl, wrapped it in cling film and put it in the fridge. I washed the tray to remove all traces of incriminating DNA and stood it on the dish rack.

I washed and wiped the marlin spike till it glinted again. I went to the study and stored it in a place that was not easily accessible.

All this violence had tired me out. I sat on my chair,

turned it so that I could put my feet up on the settee, and looked out of the window into the afternoon's blazing light.

Covert or overt? Poison or penetration? I was still dithering.

This evening, I would check out the five restaurants and bars that I had shortlisted. Perhaps the one I chose finally would help me decide the best approach to dealing with James? Hopefully one of them would ignite an epiphany?

I decided I had earned a short nap. Assassins have needs too, you know.

I went to the bedroom, drew the curtains and lay down.

CHAPTER 23

Nysa left for her meeting with Epigram at 5:00 pm. By then, I was up, all invigorated. I kissed her goodbye and saw her off at the elevator.

I decided to leave for my expedition.

Like the morning, I dressed in nondescript clothes, but of a different sort. I wore formal trousers, a beige shirt, a black blazer and leather shoes. Today was a Monday, and the restaurants and bars would be thronging with worker bees wanting to drown their blues.

What is the best way to hide? In plain sight.

I also wore my cap (I had an excuse, it was still quite sunny), my glasses and my N95 mask, which covered most of my face.

I had prepared a maroon file, inserted some papers, and clipped it shut.

Now, I was indistinguishable from the hordes.

I left the apartment, walked to the nearest MRT station and caught a train to Raffles Place. From there I walked to Lower Circular Road. It was past 6:00 pm and the place was rapidly filling up.

I walked to my first target – a dimly lit bar and eatery that claimed to be more Irish than Guinness.

I walked in explaining to the lady at the door that I was looking for some friends. The place was shaped like an L. The short leg of the L had some interesting alcoves, which I noted. I looked for the washrooms and located them. I then went to the bar and looked at the glasses they were using. I took a couple of photos with my phone.

The clientele was mostly young but there was a fair number of older men. Almost everyone was more focused on drinking; there was very little food on any of the tables.

On my way out, I looked for any sign of cameras. I couldn't spot one. That didn't mean that there weren't any, though.

I thanked the lady, explaining that I seem to have got my information wrong, and that my friends were at another bar. She barely listened, as she was busy directing a group of young thirsty friends inside.

I turned right and walked on, looking at each bar, each outlet with very different eyes than I normally would. I also looked for cameras in the street.

Within a few minutes, I came to the second target – a yellow lit space that promised authentic Mediterranean cuisine. And beer.

Here, too, the place was humming. It was a shophouse, about 20 feet wide and 40 feet deep. It was less suitable than the first – it had two rows of tables on either side of a straight aisle, and not a single nook or alcove. While it had a bar counter, it did not have seating at the bar.

I used the same excuse as before and walked in. I looked left and right, and walked towards the end, spotting the small restroom and wash area. I turned back and walked out, mentally crossing this off my list as I made my excuses with the young usher.

I walked till the end of Lower Circular Road (it is not very long) and walked back the way I came. I spotted one or two likely candidates and did a quick recce.

One of them claimed to be a sports bar and had TVs on every vertical surface to prove it. They were shaped quite interestingly, with at least two booths set in deep gloom, lit by nothing but radiation.

The other was a Mexican restaurant offering one for one cervezas till 8:00 pm. This was more brightly lit than I cared for, but offered some possibilities.

I took a few photos of each place, so that I could review my findings later, in a more conducive place. I was especially interested in the glassware. It was good to find that most restaurants used traditional glasses and mugs, not very different from each other.

As I walked to the MRT station, I evaluated the risks of using a restaurant or bar. There were clear advantages, but also some glaring disadvantages. One sharp-eyed waiter or client, and the game would be over in a snap. One slightly fumbled move, and the target would scream murder, literally.

I walked down the escalator through the station mall. Just before I took the next escalator down to the station, I noticed a small shop. More than the shop, I noticed its sign. It said,

"Party Hampers!"

Something tugged at the back of my mind.

I slowed down and walked to the shop. It was almost a cubbyhole. A smiling Filipina stood at the counter. Around her were a selection of baskets and trays with cheerfully decorated bundles of alcohol, glasses, snacks and ancillaries.

"Good evening, sir," she said, "how may I help you?"

"Ah, I was looking for…" I hesitated.

"Are you having a party? For two? For four? Or a larger group?" she asked, "we have everything you need in one hamper. No need to go to different shops for your wine or scotch, and your snacks and soda and stirrers and openers. Everything in one hamper! We also deliver!"

"May I see one?" I asked.

"Of course!" she replied enthusiastically and pushed one hamper between us on the counter.

"This one is for two people. It has a bottle of twelve-year old scotch, two sodas, two packets of peanuts and crisps, two beautiful glasses, 6 reusable plastic ice cubes…"

Have you ever been in a situation where you are facing a problem and your mind is churning continuously trying to find a solution, when suddenly, a solution that you never considered suddenly seems to pop up, neatly tied in a bow?

I have.

There is a phrase for this. It is called 'brain mining', where your brain is actually searching for and matching past situations that you have solved and then parsing the solutions and adapting them to the problem that you are currently facing.

This process doesn't look for new solutions. It reframes your challenge with the objective of finding similarities between your current problem and problems that you have dealt with and already solved. When it finds a reasonably close match, bingo! It then takes the previous solution and adapts it to your current problem.

I hope I have explained myself well.

That is what happened at "Party Hampers".

In a flash, a series of pieces fell into place.

I spent the next twenty minutes with the delightful young lady and agreed on a set of purchases. I was not carrying sufficient cash and I did not want to use my card. So, I asked her to reserve the items and said that I would pick them up the next day.

The lady was a little puzzled about two of my requests but did not allow that to dampen her desire to close the sale.

"Thank you so much, Valoma," I said, as that was her name, "You are an excellent salesperson. Your company is lucky to have you."

"Oh, thank you so much, sir," she said, "I will see you tomorrow."

I walked down one more escalator and entered the platform.

My mind was already in party mode. I cautioned it to remain calm – having a solution is quite a way away from implementing it, but it kept singing snatches of song and dancing short jigs.

Before I knew it, I had reached my destination, and about thirteen minutes later, entering my condo.

I had decided that I did not need to go to Arab Street. The solution that had presented itself did not require a bar or a restaurant.

I went up to our apartment and headed for the bar.

About six months ago, one of my consultancy clients from the US had been quite pleased with the outcomes of my efforts. I had helped them with a series of workshops that allowed them to identify causes of failure in their sales conversion, brainstorm alternate solutions and implement two of these approaches, thus yielding very positive results.

The Director responsible for Asia-Pacific had come over from Houston and had asked to meet me. We met at, where else, a bar. He was accompanied by the regional General Manager who was a business acquaintance.

"What you did was nothing short of amazing," the Director had said.

"We would like you to do this in our other regional offices," he had requested.

"We have other areas that will benefit from your interventions," he had proposed.

At the end of the evening, he presented me with an exquisitely packed case.

"You will love this," he had promised. I thanked him for his graciousness.

At home, when I opened the gift, I found two bottles of Bruichladdich X4 Quadrupled Whisky. A little pamphlet described the whisky and how it was produced using the 17th century method of quadruple distilling.

I showed them to Nysa. We agreed to open one and taste this unfamiliar spirit.

I opened it, poured a small portion each into two glasses and sat with her.

Ten seconds later, both of us were coughing and our eyes were tearing.

The whisky was almost pure alcohol! I got up, took both our glasses and poured the contents into the sink.

"Ugh," Nysa had said, "I feel that my mouth has been washed with drain cleaner! That is one drink I never hope to taste again."

The bottles remained in the bar. Untouched but not forgotten.

I rummaged and found them. I took out the unopened one.

Bruichladdich X4 Quadrupled Whisky was exactly what I needed for my plan for James Hong.

INTERLUDE 7

As Ishmael Dollah reworked his plan and somehow incorporated a complicated sounding Scotch Whisky into the latest iteration,

Inspector Julia Binti Shafiq stood in the mortuary of Tan Tock Seng Hospital, seething with anger.

Fatimavati, the abused helper, had died at 4:00 pm.

She had received the call at 4:45 pm and had rushed to the hospital.

She asked for and received an immediate meeting with the attending physician, Dr. Naidu.

"We did everything we could, Inspector," said the doctor in his soft voice. He looked tired and rumpled.

"What happened?"

"The body just gave up," he said, "Too many months of neglect and pain. Too many failing organs. Not enough strength, perhaps not enough will to live through the pain."

Julia looked at him in anguish.

"She had left her family, her home, her country," she said, her voice trembling, "so that she could earn a little money and send it back. She came to Singapore seeking a better life for her loved ones.

"And what did she get in return? Torture. Beatings. Neglect. Abuse."

Each word sounded like a hammer on dark steel.

"And now she is dead. Her husband and two children are never going to see her again. She is never going to see them again."

The doctor remained silent. His eyes did not. They spoke of his sympathy and sadness and hurt.

Julia looked at him.

"How often do you see such cases, Dr. Naidu?" she asked.

"Too often, Inspector," he said, "this is the fourth case this month, probably the fiftieth this year. In this hospital."

Julia was aghast. She knew there were many, but not to this extent.

"You mean that almost a thousand helpers are hospitalised each year?" she asked in horror.

"I would suspect more, madam, many more," said the doctor, "the figures are not shared or publicised though."

"Why not?" asked Julia angrily.

"It would be bad PR for Singapore, Inspector," said the doctor, simply.

"That is not fair!" she burst out. "Fatimavati deserves more! She deserves the government's protection. She deserves dignity. She deserves justice!"

"That is best said between you and me, Inspector," said Dr. Naidu meaningfully, "best not to shout such words aloud."

"What happens to the vermin who murdered her?" she asked knowing the truth.

"That is your domain more than mine, madam," he replied. "But you know as well as I do that the family will claim mental distress or diminished capacity, be given two to three weeks jail, and then be sent home. And the cycle will resume."

That was two hours ago.

Julia was standing outside the room Fatimavati's body lay in. She was not needed there. She wanted to be there. She had to be there.

Someone needs to stand up for her, Julia thought. No one did in life, at least I can do so in death.

She stood and thought of abuse and pain and vengeance.

CHAPTER 24

Tuesday dawned early. And bright.

I was up and on the pavement by 6:30 am. The sky was still in the throes of night, slowly warming itself in the light of the fledgling sun.

My heart rate was up, but not just because I was running.

Today, most, if not all the pieces would start coming together.

Today, the stage would be set for the next act.

I turned into Grange Road. A new condo was going up rapidly. Cement trucks lined the side of the road. I crossed to the other side, blatantly jay running.

Things to do, I thought,

One, collect the hamper from Raffles Place.

Two, collect the package from Ubi.

Three, prepare the hamper.

Four, don Serena Woo's persona and communicate with James.

Five, arrange the next steps.

All this, without killing or incriminating myself.

Piece of cake.

I turned left and ran towards the river.

What was my downside risk?

Getting caught?

Not to be arrogant or over-confident, but that possibility was very remote.

Unless something went truly, drastically wrong.

I may be suspected, yes, but caught? Unlikely.

I had spent years in the corporate world scheming and fooling and selling. I have packaged fish as fowl and vice versa. I had signed dozens of contracts that were overprized or undervalued, all in favour of the company I was working for. If I had to be caught, I would have already been.

Also, I had learnt, as CEO, not to even consider such an eventuality. Fake it till you make it, that was the name of the game.

I ran past Great World and turned right onto the riverside boardwalk.

The quietly flowing water reassured me.

If I, a glorified canal, can be marketed as a river, it seemed to say, then you can do anything you want.

I ran faster.

I reached the gates of our condo at 8:00 am. The day had taken hold, and the sun reigned in the sky.

I walked in and relished the cool air of the lobby.

Five minutes later, I was in our apartment, greeting Nysa and gulping down cold water.

"Why did you leave so early?" asked Nysa.

"I have a few things to do today," I replied, "need to get a head start. How was your meeting yesterday?"

Nysa had come back home quite late, so we really hadn't had a chance to talk.

"Oh, I think it went very well," she said, "they want me to be the lead researcher for their next three books on Singapore in the nineteenth century."

"Wow!" I said, impressed, "that's wonderful!"

"Well, nothing is signed yet," she demurred, "though they said that they are not looking at anyone else. They should be sending the draft contract later this week."

I went over to her and kissed her, being careful not to transfer any sweat.

"This is great news!" I said happily, "let's celebrate tonight!"

"No, no," she protested, "let's celebrate once the contracts are signed."

"By the way," I said, "I have reviewed Randall's agreement, and everything is in order. No surprises. You can go ahead and sign."

"Oh, good," said Nysa, "thanks, Ishmael."

"Have you told Shahed and Marianna?" I asked, "By the way, what happened? Why didn't they come over this weekend?"

"No, not yet," replied Nysa. "Marianna had called and said that they had dinner engagements on Saturday and Sunday. They met with a group of the senior partners of Nestor & Ross on Saturday, and with some friends on Sunday, I believe."

"Oh," I said, mollified.

"They will surely come over this weekend," she said.

"Great," I said, "I am off for my shower."

After a long shower and a pleasant breakfast, I set out to Raffles Place, wearing the same clothes as yesterday and retracing my route. I reached the party hamper shop at 10:15

am.

The shop was open, and Valoma was in.

"Good morning, sir," she said, "how are you today?"

"Very well, Valoma, thank you," I said, "and you?"

"All good, sir," she replied, turning and picking up a hamper. "Here, sir, one customised hamper as you specified."

She picked up another small box.

"And the glasses."

I looked over the hamper which was wrapped in unmarked clingfilm. It has all the contents that we had discussed.

"And the carry bag?" I asked.

"Here it is, sir," she said, handing me a plain brown sturdy reinforced paper bag.

"That's great, Valoma, thank you," I said gratefully, "and here is the payment, with an additional twenty dollars for you."

"Oh no, sir, that is not necessary," she protested.

"I know it is not, but I would like you to have it," I said, "you deserve it. Thank you and all the best."

I put the hamper and the glasses in the carry bag and hefted it to check if it would bear the weight. It seemed capable.

"Have a good day!" I said and walked to catch the train back to our condo.

I reached our apartment and deposited the carry bag in my wardrobe in the study.

Then, I called the number Aziz had sent me.

"Hallo? May I speak to Mr. Boon?" I asked.

"Speaking," said the voice.

"Hi, Mr. Boon, this is Mr. Aziz's friend," I said, "I understand that there is a package for me?"

"Ah, yes, sir, good morning," he replied, "the package has arrived, and it is on my desk. Should I courier it to you or would you like to pick it up?"

"I can come over, Mr. Boon," I said, "what time is convenient?"

"Any time, sir," he said, "I am here all day."

"Great," I said, "I will be there within the next hour or so."

"Sure, sir," he said, and we disconnected.

I went to Nysa's study, where she was listening to an audio book on the Anglo-Mysore wars.

I gestured to her, and she paused the program,

"Sweetheart, I have to step out for a short meeting," I said, "will be back in an hour or so."

"Okay, see you for lunch," she said.

"I'll be taking the car," I said, "is that okay?"

"Of course," said Nysa.

I left her to her martial pastime, picked up the car keys and left for Ubi.

I reached Aziz's company warehouse by noon. It was in a light industrial complex, amongst hundreds of micro and small enterprises that were the backbone of Singapore.

I parked and went up to the fourth floor, found the unit and knocked.

A young lady opened the door.

"Yes?" she asked.

"I have come to see Mr. Boon," I said, "I am Mr. Aziz's friend."

"One minute, please," she said, holding the door open. She turned around and called, "Sir, someone to see you."

A minute later, a middle-aged man came to the door,

and took over from the lady, who vanished inside. He was holding a small cardboard box liberally wrapped with sticky tape and a white A4 sized envelope.

"Mr. Boon?" I asked.

"Hallo, sir," he said, "here is the package."

"Thank you so much," I said.

"And here is the documentation along with it," he said.

"Perfect, thank you," I nodded to him, accepting both items. "Have a great day, Mr. Boon."

"You, too, sir," he said, as he closed the door.

I went back to the car, deposited the items in the backseat, and drove home.

CHAPTER 25

I entered the apartment and went straight to the study.

I placed the box in the wardrobe.

I opened my phone and sent a message to Aziz.

Package picked up.

The response was quick.

Great. Be careful.

I kept the phone down, opened the envelope and pulled out four sheets of paper.

I sat at the desk and started reading.

A Material Safety Data Sheet (MSDS) is a document that contains information on the potential hazards and how to work safely with a chemical product.

It tells one what protective equipment to wear, whether the chemical needs to be isolated from any other(s), whether the room needs ventilation and how much of it, and what are the actions one must take if something untoward happens.

The MSDS of the product that Aziz had sent me read like a biohazard warning.

When I completed it, my forehead was damp with perspiration. Yes, that may have been an effect of Singapore's notoriously humid weather, but I thought not.

I was, for the first time in a long time, afraid of an inanimate object.

I opened the topmost desk drawer and took out a scribble pad. Keeping the MSDS next to me, I wrote down what items I needed to deal with the product. I cross checked the list twice to see that I had not missed anything.

I put the MSDS sheets back into the envelope and placed in in the wardrobe.

Then I went for lunch, feeling like a condemned man.

Today's lunch was roti-prata with onion curry, followed by a sweet yoghurt dish that is one of Nysa's claims to fame.

I ate heartily. You know, the condemned man thing.

Nysa told me, with some anger in her voice, about the David-Goliath battles between Tipu Sultan and the East India Company.

"What a scheming, nasty lot they were," she said, "destroying anything that stood in the way of their profit."

I listened and nodded and ate.

Scheming and nasty were too mild for the British, I thought. There were choicer words available.

When Nysa starts a research project, she immerses herself completely. It is as if she transports into that era. As if she is there, watching, participating, feeling. Her emotions roil, her sentiments are aroused.

If she could have, she would have happily beaten Lord Cornwallis (and his various cronies) with a broom. Or a spatula. She wields both quite well.

After lunch, Nysa went back to Mysore (metaphorically) and I went to the study (literally). I picked up the list and went to our storeroom.

Many years ago, when the world was young, I was an engineer. As an engineer, I participated in many projects, some of which demanded high safety standards. So, I was used to fire-retardant, chemical-retardant coveralls, safety visors, gloves, and the like. Not only was I used to them, I had a box containing some, if not all these items. I just had to find it.

Forty dusty minutes later, I pulled out the box.

I sat down on the floor next to it. I was sixty, my back was not as flexible as it used to be and was not accustomed to bending and stretching randomly.

Opening the box, I pulled out the items one by one and checked them against my list. I found everything except two items – nitrile gloves and a bio-hazard mask.

I already had nitrile gloves in my study. I needed to get a biohazard mask or find an equivalent alternative.

Task completed, I got up, my back creaking in protest, and picked up the box and took it to the study. I deposited it next to my desk.

I opened my laptop and googled 'biohazard mask'. What would have been an anomaly some years ago was the norm in these pandemic times. Every store and its uncle sold biohazard masks including the pharmacy three blocks away.

I picked up my wallet, checked to see that I had enough cash, and walked to tell Nysa that I was stepping out for a few minutes. I also picked up my cigarettes, so that I could kill two urges with one stroll.

Fifteen minutes later, I was back, with two masks in hand and nicotine in my blood stream. I had also purchased a soft make-up brush which I would need. I deposited the masks on the box.

I went to the bar and picked up the bottle of the Bruichladdich Whisky and brought it to the study.

Now I had everything I needed to prepare the hamper.

Before I began, I again went to Nysa's room.

"So sorry," I said.

She paused the program and looked at me askingly.

"I am getting onto an important conference call," I said, "I will be locking my study door for about an hour and half. Is that okay?"

"Sure," she said, distractedly, "do you need anything? Water or a glass of juice?"

"Nothing for now, sweetheart," I said, "Just solitude."

"Ha," she said, smiling, "go ahead, I'll tell Siti not to disturb you."

"Thank you."

I closed and locked the study door and switched on the air conditioner, even though I left the bay windows wide open.

I pulled out the coveralls and shook them vigorously. The box had been packed quite well, so there was no dust or moss or any creepy crawlies.

Then, I pulled off my clothes and put them away. I wore the coveralls. I felt a moment of silly pride when they fit, pride that I was able to fit into something that I last wore more than 30 years ago. I buttoned and zipped up tight.

I then pulled the coffee table that normally sat in front of the couch and was rarely used for coffee or as a table. I brought out the hamper and the glasses and the product. I kept them on or around the table as I thought fit.

I then wore the remainder of the protective equipment – the visor, the gloves, plastic booties, a plastic haircap, the mask.

And then, heart in my mouth, I started work.

It was painstakingly slow.

It was delicate work.

The product I am referring to, as you have already inferred, was a poison. It was, as previously discussed, an ingestible poison. More than ingestible, it could actually penetrate through skin. Or be breathed in if gaseous. So many ways to die.

I had to open the bottle containing this product and transfer it. While ensuring it touched nothing else. A small amount touching the skin would result in some nasty symptoms, though not death. More than two milligrams, and you were toast.

I opened the bottle. I pushed the make-up brush into its narrow mouth. The tip of the brush grazed the surface of the colourless contents. Then, I picked up the first glass in my left hand. I pulled the brush out and coated the inside of the glass. I focused on the bottom of the glass and the lower half. I kept it aside. I picked up the second glass and repeated my actions. Ten minutes later, I again coated both glasses.

I did all this holding the glasses and brush as far away as possible from my face. It made the task cumbersome and slow. The whole process took almost one hour. I closed the bottle tight, and placed the bottle in a Ziploc bag, which I placed in another, and finally a third. I did the same with the brush.

After that, I had to repack the hamper and glasses. I used a whole box of antiseptic wet wipes to clean every possible surface I could think of. I repacked the bottle of poison, now tripled-bagged, in its original box along with the MSDS sheets and the triple bagged brush, and sealed it with even more tape than it had when I received it.

Finally, I took off the protective equipment and found myself soaking wet.

I shoved the coveralls into a plastic bag. I put the gloves, visor, booties and mask into another plastic bag.

I scanned the room to see if I had missed anything.

Then, I went for a much-needed shower.

The rest of the afternoon,

I vacuumed the study,

Took the plastic bag containing the gloves and stuff, put it into another plastic bag, and then went down to the dumpster and dropped it off,

Dropped off the coveralls at the drycleaners,

Bought new gloves, a visor, booties,

Repacked the box (without the coveralls, but with the box of poison double-wrapped in Ziploc bags) and put it back in the storeroom,

And had another shower.

On the whole, I think the afternoon had gone well.

I hadn't died. That was a good metric for success.

CHAPTER 26

That was a long day, wasn't it?

But I wasn't done yet.

After my second shower, I came to the kitchen looking for something to eat. I found Siti dicing vegetables.

"May I have something to eat, Siti?" I asked, "I'm feeling a bit hungry."

She must have been surprised but nodded unflappably, stopped cutting vegetables and washed her hands. Then she went to the refrigerator and spent a few seconds rooting inside. She emerged holding a familiar bowl wrapped in cling film.

"Some watermelon, sir?" she asked, without irony.

I recognised my victim. Adding insult to its injury, I nodded. Siti pulled of the film, put the pieces of fruit on a plate, added a fork and handed it to me.

"Thank you, Siti," I said, and went to the dining room to eat what I had killed.

After the watermelon and a drink of cool water, I was back in the study.

Time to talk to James.

I sat down, opened the laptop and logged in into Serena's account.

I spent a few minutes being Serena, liking and commenting and posting.

Then, I sent a private message to James.

Hi, James.

Thinking of you.

Hope you are having a lovely Monday.

My grandma is still in hospital, and I have taken time off to be with her.

It is so boring, and I wish I was there with you instead. But what can I do, I am dutiful and kind and sacrificing.

I look out of the hospital window yearning to see you.

A reasonable number of emojis.

It was nearing the end of the workday. I waited for a couple of minutes. Sure enough, there was James, engaging with social media instead of delivering opinions to clients, or whatever he normally did.

Hey, Serena.

So nice of you.

I've been thinking of you, too. I, too, want to be with you.

Hope your grandma is better.

I am looking forward to meeting soon, hopefully this Friday evening.

Nauseating endearments.

More emojis than a real man should be comfortable with.

I gave it a few minutes, so that Serena did not seem too eager, and then continued the conversation.

I was sweet and flattering and breathy and fluttery.

I hinted at a lot, while revealing little.

Gradually, James' metaphorical breathing quickened. I think he was becoming aroused.

After a few exchanges, I said,

One of my grandma's friends dropped off a gift hamper with some very fancy Scottish whisky.

Neither my mother nor I drink liquor.

I was wondering if I could gift this to you?

You are a man of the world, and I am sure you will appreciate this rare delicacy.

Of course, these were not the words I actually used. I mangled the sentences appropriately so that the text suited millennial IQs.

His response was immediate. The essence was,

Oh, I love Scotch. Both blended and single malt.

Just last night, my friends and I shared a bottle of Glenfiddich. It was awesome.

I would be very happy to taste the whisky and tell you about it.

Thank you so much for thinking of me.

To this, I responded,

Oh, I am so happy.

You have given meaning to my very existence.

Could you send me your address? There are a couple of people I know in the nearby HDB who are Grab drivers. I will ask one of them to deliver the hamper to you tomorrow.

What time would be most convenient?

While translating this, I conveyed my utmost gratitude that James was doing me this amazing favour.

About a minute later, James wrote,

I will be back home by 6:30 pm. Can you send it by around 7:00 pm?

I live at [Executive Condo Address in Bishan] on the eighth floor.

It is my pleasure and duty to help a damsel in distress.

I only wish I could do more to you. I mean for you.

I am counting the days till we can meet.

We went back and forth a little more. One of the things I insisted on, very sweetly, with girlish enthusiasm, was,

Please open the gift and allow the Uncle who delivers the hamper to take a photo and send it to me.

It will be like I am there with you.

Our two sundered souls will be as one.

Romeo and Juliet had nothing on us.

I am dying to see you, and by implication, be in your strong arms, while resting my comely self against your manly chest.

James agreed with enthusiasm, and reluctantly we brought the love fest to a close.

We still hadn't finalised our plan to meet.

I was hoping that we didn't have to.

I logged off, then spent a few minutes checking Google Maps to get the lay of the land in and around Bishan. I would probably have to go there once in the morning tomorrow and check out the place.

Now, I was done for the day.

I got up, stretched and left the study and went looking for Nysa.

I found her in the living room, reading one of her tomes.

"Hey, Nysa," I said.

She looked up, smiled and kept the book down.

"That was a long call," she said.

"Oh no, the call got over a while ago," I said, "they had sent over some documents that I needed to read and review."

"Epigram called," she said, "they will be sending the draft contracts tomorrow. I think this project is in the bag."

"Oh, that is wonderful!" I exclaimed, "congratulations, dearest! This is a big project, isn't it?"

"Absolutely," replied Nysa, "it's a two year assignment, at the minimum. With this and with the Randall book, I will be able to name my price for future assignments. Within reason, of course."

"Would you care for a glass of wine, milady?" I asked.

"That would be lovely, Ishmael," said Nysa, smiling.

I went to the wine cooler, fixed Nysa a glass of her favourite Rosé and handed it to her. I poured a glass for myself and toasted her.

"To the most amazing woman in the world," I said, "congratulations and kudos!"

Nysa lifted her glass, smiled and blew me a kiss.

I sat down next to her.

Both of us had had a productive day, it seemed. Time to kick back and relax.

INTERLUDE 8

As Ishmael Dollah and Nysa were celebrating their day of progress and achievement,

Inspector Julia Binti Shafiq was in the Club's main office speaking to the General Manager and getting increasingly frustrated.

"Yes, Mr. Cartwright, I understand that not all members swipe in," she said, as patiently as she could, "I also understand that the Club's system only captures those who swipe in. My question is, are there areas in the Club other than restaurants where members are required to register?"

"Well, um," said Mr. Cartwright.

Does this man start every sentence with "well, um", she wondered.

"Ah, members have to swipe when they enter the library," he said, though he sounded uncertain.

"Good," she prompted, "and where is the library?"

"Well, um," he said, "it is on the second floor, above the main lobby."

"Go on," she encouraged.

"Well, um, and the All Day Cafe," he added, "though that

does fall in the category of restaurants…"

"What All Day Cafe?" asked Julia sharply, sitting straighter.

"Well, um, it is the outlet on the first floor, adjoining the lobby," said Mr. Cartwright, "you know, the one on your right when you enter…"

"Is this next to The Olde Tavern restaurant?" she asked.

"Well, um, yes," he replied.

Julia suppressed her excitement.

"Mr. Cartwright, could you please print out the names and membership numbers of all the members who swiped into the All-Day Café on the day Mr. Closier died? Between 6:00 pm and 9:00 pm would do."

"Well, um, I would need to ask my assistant…" he started.

"Please do so now, if you don't mind," said Julia. It was not a request.

Mr. Cartwright stood up and excused himself. He left the room.

Julia was kicking herself mentally.

How did we not know about the All-Day Café? It was right next to the restaurant and the lobby. We should have looked at all the members who visited.

About ten minutes later, Mr. Cartwright entered. He had two sheets of paper in his hand.

"Well, um, here is the list of members, Inspector," he said, offering her the sheets, "I hope this is what you are looking for."

Julia practically grabbed them from him.

"Thank you," she said, as she started scanning the names.

There were about thirty or so.

She ran her eyes down the list once quickly.

Then, she went over it more carefully.

Ah.

This name sounds familiar. Why?

Dollah.

It is not a common name.

I have seen this name in connection with this case. Where?

CHAPTER 27

Sex was not on the table that night.

Only dinner was.

"So sorry, Ishmael," said Nysa, while we were eating, "I have at least another three hours of work. I have to submit a synopsis of the Anglo-Mysore wars by tomorrow morning."

I was disappointed.

I was conditioned to associate sex with wine.

Pavlov said it best - Classical conditioning refers to a learning procedure in which a biologically potent stimulus (e.g., sex) is paired with a previously neutral stimulus (e.g. a glass of wine).

I felt much like one of his dogs who responded to the bell but found no food.

I didn't express these feelings, especially at the dinner table.

"Sure, Nysa," I said, with false cheer, "I understand,"

Of course, I didn't understand.

Why on earth would Nysa choose writing a synopsis of a long-forgotten war over the prospect of a shuddering climax?

Was she faking it all this time?

Was her passion really history, rather than me?

Was our marriage real?

As I have mentioned before, we men are frail, insecure creatures.

I rose from dinner, a sadder man than when I sat down.

Nysa disappeared into her study.

I was all dressed up with nowhere to go, if you get my meaning. Wink, wink.

So, I decided to sublimate.

For those of you born after 1980, *sub·lim·ate, verb, (in psychoanalytic theory) divert or modify an instinctual impulse into a culturally higher or socially more acceptable activity.*

I picked up my iPad and opened the latest Economist.

It was not half as much fun.

I dropped off to sleep, unsated.

I woke up on Wednesday morning with a tingle in my brain.

Today was the day.

When I was running companies, seventy percent of my job was drudgery.

Approve budgets, bah!

Conduct performance appraisals, foo!

Oversee corporate audits, yawn.

Attend monthly management review meetings, Oh God, someone shoot me!

What made this seventy percent worthwhile was those few moments where we achieved something amazing. Closed a huge deal. Clinched a five-year contract. Took over a competitor who was a thorn in the side. Such times made up for all the boring, administrative stuff that CEOs have to pretend to enjoy.

Today was going to be such a signature day.

I practically jumped out of bed. Nysa was deep in sleep. I looked at her lovingly, not resenting the lack of sex the previous night a single bit.

Then I went to wash, change and hit the road.

My run seemed to go faster than usual.

The Botanical gardens shone.

Bukit Timah Road's pavement seemed springy.

I returned to our apartment by 8:30 am and found Nysa still asleep.

I glugged a litre of water and went into the shower.

Thirty minutes later, I was in the study, planning the morning recce and the evening event.

I ran through the checklist.

Gift hamper, check,

Box containing two glasses, check.

Transparent PVC gloves, check.

Marlin spike, check.

Rain poncho in pouch, check.

James' address, check.

Good. I had everything I needed. There were only two unknowns, and I would have to take a gamble on those.

Just when I was finishing, Nysa came into the room.

"Good morning," she said, sleepily, "what are you doing?"

I went to her and kissed her.

"Good morning, darling," I said, "what time did you finally get to bed?"

"Oh, it was almost 2:00 am," she said, "I want to go back to bed and sleep for another three hours."

"Synopsis done?" I asked.

"Yes, done and sent," she said.

I held her by the shoulders and steered her around.

"Go back to sleep, my love," I said, walking her to our bedroom.

"But, breakfast…" she asked.

"Siti and I have it covered, don't worry," I said.

Actually, Siti had it covered. I just removed the lids and ate.

"Thank you," she murmured and got into bed and pulled the covers over herself.

I went back to the study and did a final check.

Then, I went for breakfast.

At 10:00 am, I was on my way to Bishan.

I reached the street on which James' executive condo was and parked my car just outside one of the HDB complexes nearby. I did not enter the parking lot, as that would immediately announce my presence through the ERP card.

An executive condo is a not very common hybrid of between a public housing scheme and a private development. It is the first step up from Government housing, but not a full-fledged condominium.

The great advantage of executive condos, especially for people of my ilk, is that they do not have the ridiculous amount of security that most condos have.

I walked down the street till I came to James' building.

It was about 15 floors, a single block. As promised, there was no security.

I walked into the very basic lobby through the front entrance. I walked straight down and reached an exit in the back, which opened out into an open-air car park. I returned and saw the two elevators and a door labelled, 'management office'.

I stepped back out, went to the opposite side of the road, and looked up.

One of the unknowns resolved itself. Each apartment had a small balcony. Some of them were glassed in.

Good. The assignment could proceed.

I walked around the block. There were a couple of side streets where I could park for a few minutes without issue.

As I returned to the car, I saw a Ninja Van delivery person carry a package into James' condo. I loitered, walking slowly. Three minutes later, he was back, without the package. No security checks, no signing ins.

Good.

I looked around, searching for a shop in one of the HDBs that I thought would be useful to have as a backup. I had to walk about 100 metres, and then I saw it.

Excellent.

I returned to my car and drove back home.

The day was looking better and better.

If only there was sex.

CHAPTER 28

Nysa was still asleep when I returned.

I checked my email, pottered around the house, fixed a hinge that was squeaking. I emptied the stale water from our fountain and replenished it. I polished both pairs of my leather shoes.

I had used up all of 30 minutes.

I opened the New York Times and completed the crossword. Wednesdays were quite simple.

Then, I tried Netflix.

There was a new movie with Tom Cruise and Brad Pitt that sounded interesting.

I put it on and started watching.

Just when Tom was riding a Harley Davidson off a cliff while shooting at sundry bad guys, Nysa came in.

"Good morning," she said, brightly.

"Hey, you are up," I said, "great! I was getting bored."

"Thank you for making me go back to bed, Ishmael," she said, "I needed that."

"Cup of tea?" I asked.

"That would be lovely," she said.

I went into the kitchen and brewed Nysa a cup of her favourite ginger tea.

She took it gratefully and sipped.

"So, what is your plan for today?" I asked.

"Nothing much, actually," replied Nysa, "Once I get the draft contracts, I will need to review them. You will take a look at them for me, won't you?"

"Of course," I said, "my privilege."

"The publisher's aide may call me if they have any questions on the synopsis, but it'll most likely be an e-mail which I can respond to over the course of the day."

"What about you?" she asked.

"I have a meeting in the evening," I said, "I'll be out for a couple of hours. Is that okay?"

"Sure," said Nysa, "will you be back for dinner?"

"Yes, but only around 9:00 pm," I said, "don't wait for me, you go ahead and eat."

Nysa finished her tea.

"You continue your movie," she said, "I'll have a shower and get lunch ready."

I sat back and restarted the movie.

The Harley Davidson landed safely 300 feet below, and most of the bad guys died flaming deaths. The Harley's shock absorbers must have been really special.

By the time the movie ended, with Tom and Brad having saved the world from Armageddon, bubonic plague and Republicans, Siti was laying lunch on the table.

Nysa and I sat down to Papaya salad, Kway Teow and Mango sticky rice. The combination of flavours and textures were enough to make us want two helpings of each, ending up in feelings of lassitude and bloat.

"That was amazing," I told Nysa, as I got up and started clearing up the table. "I am the luckiest man on earth."

"I agree," said Nysa, complacently, as she carried the glasses to the sink.

On that note, I flounced out and went to our bedroom. I think I flounced, but I am not sure. It can only be noticed and appreciated by someone behind you.

I drew the curtains and collapsed on the bed.

Time for a mid-week siesta.

Just as I was dropping off, I heard the bedroom door shut, and the snick of the lock.

I opened my eyes.

Nysa stood there, next to the bed.

"You are going to get even luckier," she said, as she slipped off her blouse.

I suddenly felt very awake.

Thirty minutes later, I dropped off to sleep, with a smile on my face, and Nysa nestled against my shoulder.

Within seconds, I felt someone shaking me.

"Wha…" I sputtered.

"Ishmael, it's almost 6:00 pm," I heard Nysa's voice, "don't you have to get ready for a meeting?"

I sat up.

"Wow, 6:00 pm already?" I exclaimed, "I better rush!"

"I'll see you when you are back, sweetie," said Nysa, "I need to check my e-mails and see if the contracts have come."

"See you!" I called, as she was leaving the room.

I had a quick shower and changed into my 'nondescript' clothes, putting the mask, the specs and the baseball cap into a plastic bag.

I picked up everything I needed for the evening.

I did a final check.

Then, I left by the Utility door, as I really didn't want Nysa to ask me questions on my attire.

Siti looked at me curiously but did not comment. Her dress sense wasn't great.

I thankfully did not meet anyone in the elevator and reached the car into which I placed everything carefully in the order that they would be taken out.

I sat inside, closed the door, and did another review.

All good.

I started the car and drove to Bishan.

The traffic was heavy, but I wasn't in a hurry. I needed to be at James' place between 7:00 and 7:15 pm. I had time.

I reached James' street at 6:55 pm. I drove past the executive condo and turned into the side street I had marked in the morning.

It was quite dimly lit, which suited me fine. I couldn't spot any cameras.

I stepped out of the car and walked to the shop I had identified in the morning.

"Good evening," I said to the old lady.

She smiled and nodded.

"Pineapple tarts?" I asked. I needn't have. The whole shop was drowning in pineapple tarts.

She thought so, too. She waved her hand around, miming that I should take my pick.

I chose two boxes, paid for them in cash, and walked back to the car.

Now, if anybody asked uncomfortable questions about my presence here, I had a reason.

I put the tarts into the trunk, got into the car and geared up. I put on the specs, mask and cap. I put the poncho in my pocket. I slipped on the gloves.

I put my Oppo phone in my front pocket. I left my regular phone in the car.

The marlin spike was already taped to my left forearm with the mobile armband that Nysa had so sweetly gifted me, under the long sleeve of my t-shirt.

I picked up the bag containing the gift hamper and the box with the glasses.

I stepped out of the car and locked it.

I walked to James' condo and entered the lobby. I took the elevator to the eighth floor. I stepped out into a corridor stretching about 20 metres. There were six apartments on each floor.

The corridor was chock-a-block with shoe racks and bicycles and flowerpots. It was well lit in parts, but a couple of the lights seemed to have stopped working, so there were a couple of pools of shadow.

I walked to apartment 08-03.

I took a deep breath.

And knocked.

Thirty seconds passed. Then I heard footsteps come to the door.

It swung open, and there stood James. He was wearing a white shirt and formal grey pants. It looked like he had just returned from his office.

"Yes," he asked, though he had surmised who I was.

"Ah, Serena sent for you this package," I said, trying to sound as different from my normal speech as I could, I looked at the slip of paper on which I had written his address.

"You are James Hong?" I asked.

"Yes, I am James," he said, "please come in."

He should not have said that.

CHAPTER 29

Evidently James had ignored his parents' lessons on not talking to strangers or inviting them into his house.

I stepped in.

There was an excuse of a foyer, and then the living cum dining room.

James had walked in ahead of me.

I closed the front door and quietly latched it.

I stepped forward and moved to the living room, which had a nice settee and a coffee table in front of it, both paying homage to the 75" TV on the wall opposite.

I kept the bag on the table. I held on to the box of glasses.

"Please open." I said.

James didn't need an invitation. He pulled out the hamper from the bag.

"Wow," he crooned.

The hamper looked lovely. It was exactly like the other hampers in the shop, except that this had no markings or branding that one could spot.

The bottle of Bruichladdich whisky stood tall, its golden liquid gleaming.

James tore open the plastic wrapping.

He picked up the bottle, almost caressing it.

It was a screw top, and he twisted the cap open. He held the neck to his nose and took a deep breath.

"Aah, that smells wonderful!" he said.

"Sir, Serena said to take photo of you drinking," I said.

"Ah yes, she told me," he agreed, "let me get a glass."

"Oh no need," I reassured him, holding out the box, "she sent glasses for you. Very nice."

He kept the bottle on the coffee table and took the box from me.

It was sealed very lightly, and deliberately so. I did not need him running off looking for a knife that may serve as a weapon later.

He opened the box and took out one glass. He held it up to see if it was clean. It was. I had shined it to perfection.

He picked up the bottle and poured about 150 ml into the glass. He held it up in the air, in an imaginary toast.

By then, I had taken out the Oppo phone and was ready.

"Ready?" I asked.

"Yes," he said, and took a deep swig.

You have to give it to James, he was much better with booze than Nysa and me. He didn't even flinch.

He took a deep breath and smiled.

"Wow, that's strong!" he said.

He then put the glass to his mouth and took one more gulp.

I put the phone back in my pocket.

"You may want to sit down now," I said.

"What?" he asked.

His eyes were starting to glaze over, and a sheen of sweat

appeared on his forehead.

"Keep the glass down," I said firmly.

He obeyed and kept it on the coffee table.

"Please sit," I said.

He sat on the settee, almost collapsing into it.

"What's happening?" he asked. His voice had already begun to slur.

I was already moving.

I walked through the short corridor. On the left was a small kitchen. On the right was a small bedroom.

I reached the end. On the left was the master bedroom. On the right was a closed door, which I assumed was another bedroom or study.

I moved into the master bedroom and opened the door of the bathroom, while switching on the light.

Ah.

The bathroom had a tub.

The second unknown was resolved.

My plan had two options – one, to make it look like James took a bath when he was drunk; and two, to make it look like he lost his balance in the balcony when he was drunk. I much preferred the bathtub option. It was much more private, and it gave me enough time to clean up after me and leave without rushing. If there was no bathtub, I would have used the balcony option, but that would have meant that I would have need to expedite my exit before crowds gathered around the body and the building. Leaving a crime scene in a rush is not advisable; it may lead to leaving clues that guide the police to one's door.

I walked in.

The bathtub was quite cruddy. It was originally white

but looked brown. That in itself was sufficient cause to assassinate James. Bathtubs must always be maintained in pristine condition.

I looked for the drain plug, and pushed it in. I opened the taps and allowed water to cascade into the tub.

I came back into the living room.

James was breathing in shallow, rapid pants.

I needed to move fast. He needed to keep breathing for at least two more minutes. He needed to have water in his lungs.

I pulled out the two plastic bags from my pocket.

I carefully slipped one over his right hand and secured it with a rubber band. I did the same on his left hand.

I bent my knees, held his right arm in my left hand, and lifted him up in a fireman's carry.

I had done this many times in fire drills in my youth. I was fitter then. And people were lighter then.

James was a deadweight.

I grunted and straightened my knees with effort and stood.

I turned and walked to the bathroom, each step laborious.

I stepped in and placed him on the rim of the bathtub. The tub was half full, and the level was rising rapidly.

I lowered James into the tub, fully clothed, and arranged him with his feet towards the taps.

He was still breathing, but his eyes were closed.

I gently pushed his head down.

He slid into the water.

I shut off the taps. I waited for three minutes. No more bubbles.

I pulled out the poncho and quickly put it on.

Then, I started undressing James.

If you have never undressed a dead body in a bathtub, I strongly recommend that you keep it that way.

It wasn't easy. Or elegant. Or dry.

It took me eight minutes to get him naked.

I placed all the wet clothes in the sink.

James lay peacefully in the still water.

Time to set the stage.

Over the next six minutes,

I pulled off the plastic bags from James' hands.

I took one of his towels and wiped off the excess water from the bathroom floor. I put the towel in the sink.

Taking off the poncho, I put the wet clothes and towel into it, rolled it up, and put it in the gift hamper bag.

I used one of the plastic bags to pick up the glass that James used and put it back in the box and put the box in the gift hamper bag.

I went to the kitchen, got a glass, poured whisky in it till it was half full. I picked up a plastic stackable stool from the kitchen and took it to the bathroom and kept it next to the tub. I went to the living room and brought the glass of whisky and kept it on the stool. I smeared it a little with water.

I looked for his laundry hamper.

It was in the small bedroom, overflowing.

I pulled out a white shirt and a pair of pants and a pair of underwear.

I dropped them in a line along the corridor, hoping that it would be seen that James undressed on his way to the bathroom.

Then, I did a thorough survey of the scene.

All good.

I picked up the gift hamper bag and let myself out of the apartment.

There was no one in the corridor.

I went down by the stairs, exited the building and walked to my car.

I placed the gift hamper bag in the trunk, closed it and sat in the car. I pulled off my gloves and placed my hands on the steering wheel.

I had executed my third assignment.

INTERLUDE 9

As Ishmael Dollah was wrapping up his third assignment and the poncho with James' wet clothes,

Inspector Julia Binti Shafiq and Chee Wee were back in the conference room, poring over lists of names.

"I have seen this name before," said Julia for the umpteenth time.

"Yes, madam," said Chee Wee wearily.

It was almost 8:00 pm and he wanted to go home.

"Why can't we find it? Was it in one of the interviews with the staff? Or was it from one of the other restaurants?" she asked.

"I have not seen this name before, madam," said Chee Wee, "so I don't know."

His voice held a tinge of irritation.

Julia plopped into one of the chairs.

She slapped both hands on the table.

"It is there, somewhere," she insisted. More to herself than to Chee Wee.

Am I mixing names from two different cases? She wondered.

Her eyes felt grainy. She rubbed them, to no avail.

"Okay Chee Wee, go on, its late," she said, "let's deal with this tomorrow."

Chee Wee's face lit up.

"Thank you, madam," he said, and scurried out of the room before Julia could change her mind.

Julia stood and collected all the lists into one pile. She shoved the papers into a blue file. She walked to the door, put off the AC and lights and left the room.

She walked down the corridor to her temporary office, entered it and threw the file on her desk.

Dollah.

I have seen this name, she said to herself.

Julia leaned over and shut down her computer. Then, she picked up her tote, put off the lights and exited the office. She shut the door and locked it.

She walked to the elevator, while fumbling for her cigarettes.

As she walked towards the smoking area, a second name floated into her mind.

Marianne? Mary Anne? Marianna?

Marianna Dollah – that was the name. Not Ishmael. Marianna Dollah.

Who was Marianna Dollah?

She stopped and pulled out her phone.

She opened the browser and typed, 'Marianna Dollah LinkedIn'.

The browser responded.

"Yes!" she cried, startling the officer walking towards the parking lot.

"Yes! I knew it!"

Marianna Dollah, partner with Nestor & Ross.

Here was the connection.

Julia slipped her phone back into her pocket and walked with a confident stride to smoke her well-deserved cigarette.

CHAPTER 30

I sat unmoving in the car for about three minutes.

It was 7:40 pm.

I had been in James's apartment for less than 30 minutes.

I started the engine and drove away.

First, I drove towards Ang Mo Kio, rather than back home.

I reached a food court and parked the car in the lot.

I went in and ordered three servings of Laksa. I asked for them to be given in three separate plastic bags.

Ten quick minutes later, I carried the bags back to the car.

I opened the trunk. I kept two of the bags down next to the car. I opened the Laksa container in the third bag and poured it into the bag.

I picked up the gloves from the front seat and wore them again. I carefully opened the poncho wrapping and pulled out James' shirt and underwear.

I dropped them into the bag with the Laksa.

I tied it tight. I walked to the garbage bin just outside the food court and dropped the bag into it.

I came back to the car and placed the other two Laksas in the back seat well.

I drove out of the food court car park and to another food court in Thompson Road.

I repeated the exercise with James' pants.

I drove to a third food court in Seletar Green and disposed the towel with the third Laksa.

Finally, I drove to a small alley near Pierce Reservoir. I had run past this before, at night. It was dark, mostly empty and quite quiet.

I took out the box containing the glasses.

I kept it on the ground and stepped on it hard. I could hear the glasses cracking. I stamped four or five times, till I was sure that glasses were fragmented. I picked the box and placed it in a plastic bag. I tied it tight and walked to a garbage bin that was overflowing with wet waste. I pushed the plastic bag in as deep as it could go.

Then, I pulled off the gloves and dropped one each in different bins on the lane on the way back to the car.

From Pierce Reservoir, I drove past Upper Thompson mall, stopped briefly at the bus stop, rolled up the poncho and deposited it in a garbage bin.

I checked the car and trunk once for good measure.

Finally, I drove home.

I reached our condo at 9:55 pm.

In the basement carpark, I removed the mask, the cap and the specs. I rolled them up in a tight bundle and put them into the gift hamper bag. I checked the car. It seemed clean. I made a note to arrange to wash it and vacuum the interiors the next day.

I picked up the gift hamper bag as well as the plastic bag

containing the pineapple tarts I had purchased earlier, went to the elevator and rose to the 24th floor.

My legs were hurting, and my knees were almost giving way. My back was protesting creakily about the indignities that I had subjected it to; like me, it was retired and was not prepared for such harsh treatment.

I entered our apartment and moved as quickly as possible to the study. I reached there without being accosted.

I quickly undressed. I pulled out a plastic bag from one of the desk drawers (yes, I save them) and dropped all the clothes I was wearing into it. I then placed the plastic bag in the gift hamper bag.

I untaped the marlin spike from my forearm and placed that in the gift hamper bag, too. I then took a long, hot shower, cleaning away any traces of residue and giving my muscles some surcease.

"Ishmael, is that you?" I heard Nysa call.

I stepped out of the shower, wrapped in my towel.

"Yes, dear," I called back, "just got back."

"Dinner is on the table," she said, "I will just join you in a minute."

Donning my shorts and a t-shirt, I tucked away the bag containing the debris of my evening into the recesses of my wardrobe and went to the dining room, carrying the pineapple tarts with me.

En route, I walked into the kitchen, said hi to Siti and handed over the tarts.

The table was laid.

Dinner was usually light – a salad, some veggies, a bowl of soup or lentils, and yoghurt.

I sat down and opened the bowl containing diced fruit.

I picked up a fork and started eating directly from the bowl.

Just when I was picking up the third piece of pineapple, I felt a sharp rap on the back of my head.

"How many times have I told you not to eat directly from the bowl?" asked Nysa, in an irritated voice.

"I was hungry," I whined.

"You have your plate and bowl in front of you," she retorted, "can't you take a minute to serve yourself and eat like a civilised person?"

"No, I can't," I muttered rebelliously sotto voce, while serving the fruit into my bowl.

Nysa sat across me.

"How was your meeting?" she asked, as she served herself.

"Good, but tiring," I said honestly.

"You say you are retired, but you keep running around more than you did when you were working full time," she observed.

"Just trying to stay relevant, that's all," I said, "I don't want to fade away too quickly."

"Are you missing work?" she asked, gently. Nysa is more perceptive than is good for me.

"Umm, sometimes," I replied.

"Maybe you should look for a steady pastime," she said, "one that keeps you engaged on a regular basis. One where you can use all the knowledge and skills you have accumulated over the past decades."

See? How perceptive? She cuts too close to the bone sometimes.

"That is a good idea," I said, consideringly, "let me give it some thought."

"By the way, why are you eating now?" I asked, "I thought I told you not to wait up."

"Yes, my lord," she said, smiling, "I am sorry I disobeyed you, my lord."

What do you do with a problem like Nysa?

After dinner, Nysa put everything away and I washed the dishes and dried them. (It was well past Siti's bedtime)

"Did you receive the draft contracts from Epigram?" I asked Nysa. "How were they?"

"Oh yes, I did," she replied, "just glanced through them. So far, they seem fine, but I need you to review them, too."

"Tomorrow can?" I asked.

"Of course," she said, as she wiped her hands dry on the kitchen towel.

We put off the lights and headed to bed.

"What do you want to watch?" asked Nysa, putting on the TV.

"Anything," I said, "I am not fussed."

These days, Nysa's default program was The Crown.

As we watched the Prince and Princess of Wales betray each other in unseemly ways, I edged closer to Nysa and ran my fingers down her arm.

"Why, Ishmael," she said, "wasn't the afternoon enough? We aren't in our thirties anymore!"

I am nothing if not persistent. I continued exploring further, and her body's reactions belied her words.

Soon she turned away from the Royal Family and gave herself up to my caresses.

I paused in my administrations and switched off the TV.

That night, we gave our thirty-year old selves a run for their money.

CHAPTER 31

I woke up on Thursday feeling every year of my sixty in every part of my body.

Nysa was already up and about.

I stretched gingerly. My muscles sent me messages that were not suited for general audiences.

I blamed Nysa.

Didn't she have any consideration for her aging husband? Shouldn't she stop making unnecessary demands on his frail body?

I blamed her while smiling like a Cheshire cat. That ate the cream. And Tweety Bird.

I blamed her while patting myself on the back. Way to go, Ishmael, not bad for an old man, huh?

I arose and limped to the bathroom.

After a slow and leisurely brush and wash, my body started forgiving my excesses.

I stepped into my study.

Should I? Shouldn't I?

I should. I put on my running gear.

I went to the kitchen to have my two glasses of water.

"Good morning, Siti," I said, as I filled my glass from the sink tap, "have you seen Nysa madam?"

"Good morning, sir," she replied, "yes, madam in her room."

"Thank you," I said, and made my way to Nysa's study / library / messiest place in the house.

I knocked and pushed the door open.

Nysa was at her desk with her laptop open.

"Good morning, sweetheart," I said.

She looked up and smiled. It was a knowing smile.

"Did you sleep well?" she asked, knowing the answer.

"Not at all," I said, with a chuckle.

"I am off for my run," I continued, "may I review your contracts when I am back?"

"How you have the energy to run after yesterday, I cannot imagine!" said Nysa, in a mock-indignant tone, "but if you must, go ahead. Yes, we can review the contracts once you are back."

I bent down, kissed her and left her room.

I took the elevator to the lobby and started with walking around the condo. I needed my muscles to stretch and warm up – they were still unhappy about the demands placed on them yesterday.

After about five rounds, I stepped out of the condo and turned right. Kallang River, here I come.

The first hundred metres were brutal. As were the next and the next. Gritting my teeth, I ran through the pain and left it behind me.

Let us review last night, I thought, as the pavement tiles receded two at a time under my feet.

Were there any shortfalls in planning?

Yes.

One, I didn't know whether there were any cameras, and if so, where they were.

Two, I went into James' house not knowing if it had a bathtub, which was a big part of the execution.

Three, I would have been in trouble if he had been expecting someone, which I had no idea about.

Four, I needed a much better 'disposal' process. What I did last night, moving from food court to food court was suboptimal, to say the least.

All in all, if I were to achieve consistent results in my new profession, I needed more and better information about the targets and their ecosystems.

Were there any shortfalls in execution?

In general, no.

Everything went as planned.

However, James could have recognised me from our meeting at the Nestor & Ross party. Should I have altered my appearance a little?

Something to think about.

However, I would have to wait and see. Would the death be registered as a homicide or an accidental death? The proof of any pudding lies in the aftertaste.

Post execution wrap up?

I could have taken a few more bags and rubber bands.

I could have taken a cleaning solvent and some rags. I can't depend on these being available with the target.

I was uncomfortable driving our car to the target's vicinity. A thorough investigation could raise questions about my presence. How many times could I buy pineapple tarts? Should I use some other form of transportation?

What?

I could have been spotted leaving James' condo. Or returning to ours, dressed very unlike how I am normally seen. Do I need a staging area?

I turned into the riverbank.

My muscles were shrieking again. You can't do this to us! This is abuse!

I slowed down to a walk.

There were dozens of scullers in the river, slicing through the calm waters. Some of them were alone, some in couples and a few in groups.

On the left, a group of geriatrics were moving slowly in rhythm, practicing Tai Chi. I knew that this was a great exercise regime, but it looked quite hilarious, as if everyone were moving in slow motion.

I walked for about 300 metres and then resumed jogging.

At the end of the promenade, I turned around and made my way back to our condo.

How would I know the progress of the police investigation?

There were too many gaps for comfort.

I needed to build a team. Especially if I was to move from amateur to professional.

The team, in my reckoning, needed at least three members.

First, it needed someone with inroads into the police department. Someone who could access cameras and reports and inside information.

Second, it needed someone with digital skills, who could access information not found in public sources.

And third, it needed someone who could handle logistics

– purchases and transportation and clothing and so on.

Assassination by itself is a solitary endeavour. But the preparation, planning and aftermath needs support.

Finding and putting together such a team was not going to be easy.

It was not going to be cheap.

There was the risk of one member letting the team down or betraying all of us.

In life, every pro seems to have a con.

But without a team, the gaps and the risks were too large. It was clear that it was unadvisable to take assassination up as a vocation while playing solo. The probability of failure or capture was unsustainably high.

I finally reached the last lap. Unfortunately, our condo sits on a small rise, and the last lap was all uphill.

It took everything not to stop.

When I trundled through our gates, I felt like Pheidippides completing the marathon. Yes, I felt like I was dying.

I reached the elevator and leaned gratefully against its side. I was smearing the polished steel with my sweat but did not care.

I reached our apartment. By then, my breathing had calmed to a steady pant.

I took off my shoes and walked in, heading for the kitchen to get some water.

As I entered the dining room, Nysa came out of the kitchen, her phone against her ear.

She held her hand up, gesturing for me to stop.

"Just a minute, Ishmael has just entered," she said, "let me put you on speakerphone."

She pressed a button on the screen.

"Who is it?" I asked, not happy at being ambushed like this.

"It's me, Marianna," said the phone in response.

"Hi Marianna, what's up? How are you guys doing?" I asked.

"You sound like you are panting," said Marianna, her voice concerned.

"Yes, just returned from my run," I said. "So, tell me, what's up?

"Ishmael," she said, in a sober voice, "James Hong is dead."

CHAPTER 32

The words echoed in the dining room.

"What?" I asked, in shock, "Dead? How? He must be quite young, right? You said he was just an associate."

"Yes, he was young, just about my age or a couple of years older," she replied, "it was a shock to all of us."

"What happened?" I asked again.

"No one knows for sure, Ishmael," she replied, "we hear that he died in his apartment, drowned in his tub. But this is not confirmed."

"Oh," I said, "have the police said anything?"

"I believe that a senior officer spoke to Richard," she said, referring to her Managing Partner.

Nysa stepped in.

"Isn't this the person who was causing you trouble, Anna?" she asked.

"Yes, Nysa," she said, "James was spreading rumours about me and hurting my chances with the Board."

"Then, good riddance!" said Nysa, firmly.

"Nysa!" exclaimed Marianna, in a shocked voice.

"What?" she said, unapologetically, "No one hurts my

child and gets away. This is Karma!"

"Nysa," said Marianna, again, but with less insistence.

"Ok, guys, sorry to hear this, but I really need some water," I said, "I am dying of thirst."

"You go ahead," said Nysa, "I'll talk to Marianna."

I went into the kitchen and downed three glasses of water.

Ahhh.

I then went into the Utility room and washed my face in the sink. I could feel my skin rehydrating thirstily.

When I came out, Nysa was on the couch, continuing to speak to Marianna.

I waved at her and went to the study, stepped out of my running clothes and went for a shower.

Fifteen minutes later, I emerged a new man. I went to the dining room in search of breakfast. Nysa had completed her call and was at the table waiting for me. She had served watermelon and oranges in two bowls.

I dug in, shovelling the pieces of fruit into my mouth in rapid succession.

Nysa ate more circumspectly.

"This is the second death in Marianna's company," she said, worriedly, "what is wrong? Is there some sort of curse on them?"

The fruit in my mouth gave me time to think. I swallowed and said,

"This happens sometimes, Nysa. Do you recall, in 1998, my friend Dharmesh's employees going on a day trip and their bus capsizing? Four or five employees died, if I remember right."

"Yes, I remember," she said, her voice sad, "You had

gone to help with organising the ambulance and mortuary and stuff. That was such a terrible situation."

"Also, when I was in Metrocyn," I said, "we lost Graham Johnson to a heart attack, and Eric Tang to a stroke, and Thelma Soong to cancer. All in the space of 3-4 months, I think."

"Yes, I remember," she said.

"Death is a norm," I said, "we just don't hear of it or see it because we are removed by a couple of degrees of separation. In the case of Marianna's firm, there is no separation. So, we see it as an anomaly."

"Anyway, I mean what I said earlier," she said, her eyes flashing a little, "I am sad that this James is dead and feel for his family, but if he was the one causing our Marianna trouble, I am also glad!"

And I am glad that you feel this way, my dear, I thought, without uttering the words.

We finished breakfast, and I followed Nysa to her study.

"May I review the contracts now?" I asked, "should I do it on your computer, or would you like to send them to me?"

"Oh, please do it on mine," she replied, "and take me through the points so that I know how to explain them to the publishers legal counsel."

"Of course," I said.

Nysa opened the documents for me on her laptop and vacated her chair.

I sat down and started reading.

There were two contracts, the first one dealing with the terms and conditions of the engagement, and the second with disclosure and usage of the research product.

It took me about half hour to go through the drafts. They

were quite straightforward. I highlighted areas of ambiguity – there were only a couple – and underlined a few errors.

I called Nysa over and showed her my comments and the reasons behind them.

"Thank you, Ishmael," she said, "I will ask for a call later today or tomorrow and finalise these."

She picked up her phone and started drafting a WhatsApp message.

"Well done, Nysa," I said, smiling happily for her, "this will put you on the map, for sure."

"About time, too," she said, looking up, "it's been more than ten years of effort, and any recognition is most welcome."

I left her to her devices, electronic and otherwise, and went to my study. I still had a few things to do to close the James Hong assignment.

First, I went into Facebook and logged on to Serena's account. I sent a couple of messages to James. First, asking whether he had liked my gift and the second, fifteen minutes later, asking why he was not responding.

I kept that conversation pending and moved to the gift hamper bag.

I removed the plastic bag with my clothes and went to the Utility room. The washing machine was empty. I dropped the clothes in, added twice the normal amount of soap and put the water on its highest temperature setting.

I then went to our shoe shelf, just inside the front door, took out the walking shoes I was wearing the previous night, and took them to the guest bathroom. There, I washed the shoes, soaped them with the hand soap, rinsed them and put them by the windowsill to dry.

I went back to the study, pulled out another plastic bag and stuffed the mask and cap into it. I went to the kitchen and opened the garbage bin. There were watermelon peels, eggshells and some vegetable cuttings. I scooped some of them and put them in the bag with the mask and cap, tied it shut, and threw it into the chute. I washed my hands.

Once again to the study. I picked up a pair of scissors and cut the gift hamper bag into small pieces and put them in yet another plastic bag. I went to the kitchen, repeated the exercise with the remaining organic matter in the garbage bin, and threw the plastic bag into the chute. I washed my hands again.

The washing machine was still whirring and sloshing.

I returned to the laptop.

I checked my e-mails and responded to a couple.

After half hour had passed, I became a very pissed off Serena.

I sent a nasty message to James, without a single emoji, told him that he was an ungrateful cad and an unimaginable rotter of the highest order. As a climax to that tirade, I unfriended him.

Then I deleted the Facebook account. Next, I went into the normally unvisited sectors of my computer hard drive and deleted it again. Would there be traces? Of course. Nothing is ever truly gone. But they would be very hard to find.

I leaned back in my chair. I went through everything once again. Had I thoroughly expunged any trace of my visit to James' condo?

I believed so.

If at all I was asked why my car was parked or seen in the

vicinity, I could say that I was returning from shopping in Ang Mo Kio and stopped to buy Singapore's best pineapple tarts.

I went to the washing machine and pulled out the clothes and dropped them into the dryer, once again setting the temperature at its maximum.

Once the clothes were dry, I would fold them, pack them and put them away in the suitcase earmarked for donations meant for Salvation Army.

I picked up the marlin spike and tucked it away carefully. Its time would come.

I picked up my iPad, sat on the settee and read till lunch.

INTERLUDE 10

As Ishmael Dollah was getting rid of the last traces of any evidence of his visit to James Hong's condo,

Inspector Julia Binti Shafiq was in her temporary office on a call with her soon to be ex-husband.

"No, I don't want to meet you," she said.

"Please, Julie," begged Aman, "just for a cup of coffee. Wherever you say. Just once."

"Sorry, Aman, no." her voice was firm and final.

"Why are you like this?" he whined, "we were husband and wife for twelve years…"

Julia cut him off.

"And you beat me for four of those years," she said coldly, holding back her sorrow and rage.

"I have changed, Julie," said Aman, sincerely, "I realise my mistakes. I am different now."

"Bullshit," said Julia crisply. "That's what you said after every time you knocked me around. That's what you said when I wanted us to go to a marriage counsellor. You have not changed. You cannot change."

"I have been having sessions with a psychiatrist," said

Aman, "and she has been very helpful. I really have changed, Julie, promise."

"Good," she said, "I hope you feel better. I hope you have a good life. Goodbye."

"Wait, wait, please wait, Julie," pleaded Aman, desperation in his voice.

"There is nothing to talk about, Aman," said Julia. "We are done. Goodbye."

She cut off the call.

Then, she lowered her head onto her arms on the table.

How did a sweet, introverted, smart young boy become a nasty, abusive, wife-beating monster?

At first, it was all sweetness and light. All laughter and love.

Then, the whines about things not going well at work. About horrid bosses and back-stabbing colleagues. Followed by the fights about small things.

Then the occasional drink, just to 'fit in with the boys'.

Leading to coming home at midnight, staggering, slobbering, stinking.

Then the fights about bigger things.

Each time, remorse and apologies and forgiveness and promises.

Till the first slap.

That came as a complete shock.

Never in her wildest dreams did she imagine that Aman, her Aman, would lift a hand against her. He was always, even at his worst, her hero, her protector.

She was at a complete loss. She had no idea how to respond.

Aman walked out of the house and didn't return till the

next day. When he did, it was with flowers and apologies.

"I don't know what came over me, Julie?"

"I must be insane to do something like that to the love of my life."

A month later, another slap. Then two.

A shove. A pull of her hair. A fist into her stomach.

What do you do when the person you adore attacks you?

What do you do when your best friend betrays you?

What do you do when your shield cuts you?

Julia's head came up, proud and erect.

I will leverage my pain, she thought. I know what it is to be a victim.

I will do everything I can to catch and punish the Amans of the world and make them pay.

CHAPTER 33

Shahed called when Nysa and I were having lunch.
He was in KL, on a business trip.

I put him on speaker.

"You must have heard, Dad, about James Hong?" he said.

"Yes, Shahed, Marianna called Mummy earlier this morning," I said, "it was a shock."

"This is the second death in Marianna's firm in less than a month," he said, "I was wondering if they are cursed or something."

"You are your mother's son," I smiled, "she said exactly the same thing."

"Of course, he is my son," said Nysa, "and I am his favourite parent."

"Do you know what happened, Shahed?" I asked, "All we know is that he drowned or something. Was he swimming?"

"No, it seems he was drinking while having a bath in his tub," said Shahed, "and then drowned. That's all I know."

"Wow, he must have been really drunk," I said, "almost to the point of unconsciousness."

"It's really weird," said Shahed, "first Greg and then James. I am worried that nothing should happen…"

"Don't worry, Shahed," said Nysa, soothingly, "nothing will happen to Marianna. We are here, aren't we?"

"So, when are you back?" I asked, leading Shahed to a happier topic.

We spoke for a couple of minutes more and said our goodbyes.

Nysa looked at me in concern.

"Should we ask Marianna to look for another job, Ishmael?" she asked, frowning.

'Don't be silly', I was just about to say. I restrained myself.

"Why don't we all talk when we meet over the weekend?" I said, with much more tact than I am normally known for. "Let's see what Marianna feels."

After polishing of the amazing appams and stew and having two helpings of the mango parfait, I went to the study.

On my way, I collected the dry clothes. I folded them and put them in a plastic bag, to put away in the donations suitcase.

Then, I fired up my laptop and opened the browser.

"Rahul Sinha LinkedIn", I typed.

I spent the next two hours learning everything I could know about Rahul.

First by overt means and then by not so overt means.

On the surface, Rahul Sinha came across as an exemplary professional, with a meteoric career graph, recommendations by the rich and famous, with a network that was studded with A-listers and prominent members of society.

As I dug deeper, a different picture emerged.

Rahul was a defendant in eleven wrongful termination cases. He was a defendant in two sexual harassment cases. All of these were settled and suppressed.

He was named and shamed in Glass door as a 'horrible, hateful manager' and a 'tyrant and bully'.

None of his subordinates was a connection on LinkedIn. Only peers and superiors.

His posts were a mix of subservience and condescension, of not so humble bragging.

He had an ongoing case against him – a complaint by a security guard in his condo whom he berated and threatened.

On the whole, not a person who should be given charge of a department, let alone a company.

As I read, I felt my anger building.

Rahul Sinha had been given everything.

He was born in a rich family. He attended the best schools in India and graduated from an Ivy League College. He sought and won prime jobs in reputed companies. He had had access to power and privilege from when he was young.

And instead of using all these advantages to create value, to distribute largesse to those less fortunate, he had spent his adult life taking, hurting, bullying, abusing, shaming.

I leaned back in my chair. My mind spiralled into the past.

I had made many mistakes in my career. Some of them insignificant, some of them cringe worthy, and a few real humdingers.

One of the worst mistakes I had made was in Metrocyn.

I had been invited by the Board to take over an ailing company from a tired, indifferent CEO. He had lost all interest and had already retired in his mind.

Before he left, he gave me his cursory views on the senior management team. As always, I listened carefully and made notes.

"I suggest you get rid of John Choo, the CFO," he had said. "He is very good at his job but is toxic to the company."

Unfortunately, I had already judged the CEO and found him wanting. So, I did not give his comments the respect they deserved.

Also, on first glance, I had found the CFO to be knowledgeable and charming. He was cooperative and diligent.

I dismissed the CEO's comments and forgot about them.

A few months passed, in a whirlwind of cost cutting and rightsizing. I was working fourteen to sixteen hour days, trying to stem the bleeding of a company in its last throes.

Gradually, ever so slowly, we were pulling back from the brink.

Then, in dribs and drabs, I heard about the CFO from various sources.

His nastiness. His bullying tactics. His calls to Board members couching complaints as 'raising issues before they became problems'. His influencing his team to follow his lead and ape his behaviour.

For a CEO battling liquidation, a CFO is very important. Critical, even, to keep the banks and creditors on side. I considered what I heard, but decided to take the expedient path, and did nothing.

The trickles grew to torrents that grew to floods.

Good people started leaving, first in ones and twos, and then in groups.

The CFO's team began mirroring their boss and became sources of toxicity themselves. Whole departments became reluctant to deal with the Finance team.

Then, I started getting calls from Board members. Calls that evinced concern, but that had quasi-facts that seemed like I was driving the company over the edge.

I took a break from operations and spent two days collaring each of the seven Board members. A pattern emerged – John Choo said this, John Choo was concerned that, John Choo feels that this decision you made was, John Choo said the banks were worried about…

I asked for an emergency Board meeting. It was just the Board and me.

I presented what we had done in the last nine months. I showed them where we really were when I began, and where we were now. I took them along the path that I saw for the company twelve months from now.

Then, I offered my resignation. I am happy to leave, I said, if the Board does not have confidence in me. I serve at their pleasure, I said.

They asked me for fifteen minutes. When I returned to the conference room, they offered me their unconditional support.

I thanked them.

When I left the conference room, I walked to John Choo's office and fired him. I asked him to leave the office immediately.

He created a huge scene. He would sue for wrongful termination, he shouted. He would make sure that the banks would foreclose on us, he threatened. He would destroy me, my reputation and my life, he promised.

I saw him to the door and watched him walk away.

I had finally done the right thing, but it was almost too late.

For the next two months I battled the repercussions of having left the cancer untreated for too long. The finance team, at least that part loyal to John, resigned en masse. The banks called and expressed their fears. Investors raised questions.

Step by miserable step, day by difficult day, we stabilised the company. It took almost three months to sort out all the internal issues and bring us back to even keel.

When I next met the former CEO, I apologised. I am sorry I disregarded your advice, I said.

I am sorry, too, he said. I should have fired John much before, but was too tired to deal with it, and so left the problem for you to resolve.

We shook hands and forgave each other.

But I never forgave myself. I had inflicted so much harm on the company because I took the easy path. Yes, in the next twelve months, Metrocyn recovered. The company grew, gradually became the stock market's darling and its shareholders' golden goose. But that did not take away the pain and suffering I had caused.

Rahul Sinha was another John Choo.

It was time for redemption.

CHAPTER 34

It was 5:00 pm by the time I closed the laptop. I got up and stretched away the kinks.

I went up to the balcony and lit a cigarette. As I smoked, I looked out at what was arguably the most beautiful island in the world. The sun's rays slid from left to right. Half of what I could see shone like gold; the other half lurked in dark shadows. Yin and Yang, I thought.

So, Rahul Sinha.

He was not going to be easy to get to, unlike James Hong.

Rahul lived in the Marina Sail, a high-end condo in the central business district. It was sure to be bristling with cameras and security guards.

The good thing was that Rahul lived alone. He was divorced and did not seem to have a current partner.

Rahul and I shared some mutual connections (seventeen according to LinkedIn, including Derek Francis) but none who could engineer a casual meeting.

I would have to not just think out of the box on this assignment. I would have to think outside the room the box was in.

But before that, I needed to speak to Derek. I needed to know what happened to the seven former employees who left because of Rahul. I had no idea whether Derek or his HR team would have kept track, but I hoped so.

I sent a WhatsApp message to Derek,

Hey Derek, let me know when you would be free for a brief chat.

Two minutes later, I received,

Now?

I called him.

"Derek," I said, after we had completed the pleasantries, "as per the file you shared with me, seven employees left due to the person in question. Do we have any information of where they are now and what they are doing?"

His response was immediate.

"Yes, we do," he said, "our HR team has been communicating with them and helping them."

"That's good," I said, "Is there someone who could put together a brief report on these seven, and share it with me?"

"Of course," said Derek, "I will have it sent to you by close of business tomorrow."

"Thank you so much, Derek," I said, and signed off.

I left the balcony and went to Nysa's room.

She was at her desk.

I checked if she was on a call. She wasn't.

"I am stepping out for a walk, sweetie," I said, "Be back in about an hour."

"Okay, bye," she said, waving.

I changed into my running gear and set out.

As I left our condo, I started my analysis.

Who is the target – Rahul Sinha of Jetsmart.

Why is Rahul Sinha a target – for all the reasons stated before – he detracts value from the world around him, is toxic, hurts people, and is a threat to Derek who is my friend.

What is the desired outcome – the ideal outcome may be one where he leaves the company of his own accord and changes his behaviour in the future. However, that is unlikely and reversible. Thus, the optimal solution is a permanent one.

Where is the best place – not sure but will be outside his place of work or home, as it would be difficult to get to him at his office or home. Restaurant? Bar? Club?

When is the ideal time – not sure, but likely to be in the evening, after working hours.

How (method of elimination) – not sure but will need to be something that can be used in a public location without creating a ruckus.

I turned and twisted each point, testing new limits.

What were the constraints?

Rahul seemed smarter than James, it was unlikely that he would be easily catfished. Also, it was not safe to use the same method twice within a short space of time.

I had no direct connects to Rahul. Also, it was unadvisable that I, a friend of Derek, was seen in his company shortly before a tragic outcome.

He was inaccessible in his office and his home.

What weighed in my favour?

Very little.

Rahul was ambitious and hungry.

He was widely disliked, so the suspect pool would be quite vast.

Where was he most vulnerable?

Good question. This needed more research. The question could also be reworded as – where and when was he alone? How often and how long?

I looked around me. I had reached Middle Road. Time to head back.

I walked towards Bras Basah.

Reviewing all the points evaluated so far, I decided to examine the 'how' further.

The 'sharp thin object into brain' approach seemed to have worked well with Lee. It was appropriate as Lee was older, slower and not aware of his surroundings.

The 'poison in the glass' approach was right for James. Here he was so besotted with Serena and so excited to get a gift from a girl he barely knew, he didn't pause to question or think.

Also, coroners were not fools. Sooner or later, they would ask questions about the parade of bodies filing through their cabinets. Examinations and autopsies would become more thorough.

What was the most common type of fatal accident in Singapore? I would Google that when I returned. This assignment needed to be a common accident, one that was not questioned.

Much of my working life was spent in analysis.

When I was in the fledgling stages of my career, an early mentor taught me this method.

The "5W1H approach" or "Kipling method" asks a list of fundamental questions,

What? Why? Who? Where? When? and How?

whose answers are considered necessary for analysis, problem-solving, decision making, and opportunity analysis.

I learnt later on that this method is widely used across the world in police investigations, brain-storming exercises and research projects.

Why was it called the Kipling method, I had wondered, and spent time to find the answer.

I found out that the author Rudyard Kipling had pioneered this approach in his "Just So Stories".

A poem accompanying the tale of "The Elephant's Child" opens with:

"I keep six honest serving-men
They taught me all I knew;
Their names are What and Why and When and How and Where
and Who."

I had learnt to always started with 'why' or 'who'. Once that foundational question was answered, the other questions had a broad direction, which made them less cumbersome, if not actually easier, to answer.

Applying this method to assassination may not have been the best approach, but it is the one I had and was used to. Also, I don't believe there was a handbook for assassins that laid out a decision tree for differing circumstances. Each case was unique and needed to be analysed and evaluated without bias or preconception.

The process had begun. I just needed a few more iterations to reach the decisions I needed.

I walked into our condo. It was almost 7:00 pm. Two of our neighbours were in the lobby speaking to one another.

I smiled, wished them a good evening, and walked to the elevator.

I was hungry. Analysis burnt more calories than nutritionists believed.

I walked into our apartment and was going to call out to Nysa, when I noticed a familiar pair of heels outside the door.

Marianna was visiting.

CHAPTER 35

She was in the living room.

"Hi, Marianna," I said, happy to see her.

"Hi, Ishmael," she said, smiling, and got up to give me a hug.

"Why are you sitting alone?" I asked, "where is Nysa?"

"In the kitchen, making tea," said Marianna, "Siti has gone out to buy vegetables, so…"

"Will you be having dinner with us?" I asked.

"Of course, she will," said Nysa, as she walked in with a tray holding a teapot, two cups on saucers and a small container of milk.

"That's great," I said, as I took the tray from Nysa and placed it on the centre table.

I poured the tea into the cups, asked about and added milk and handed the cups to the two ladies. I then sat next to Nysa.

"Thank you, I needed that," said Marianna, after she took a sip.

"Marianna is here to discuss Shahed's surprise party," said Nysa, in a no-nonsense tone, daring me to object.

I didn't.

I have learned to pick my battles. A surprise party is not a hill I want to die on.

"Mm-hmm," I said.

"As Nysa may have told you, I have booked the Tourmaline Ball Room at the US Club," said Marianna. "I have told Shahed that I have booked a table for two at the Club's Italian restaurant, Providore, for 7:00 pm."

"Good idea," said Nysa, approvingly, "he will come to the club without suspecting anything."

"Yes," said Marianna, smiling slyly.

"I have invited about fifty friends," she continued, "and forty-five have confirmed. Then there's both of you and my Dad, who's coming over from KL."

"Oh, that's great," I said, "it's been a while since we met Kabir!"

"The Club will do the catering," said Marianna, "and we can get our own liquor, but they will charge corkage."

"I can help with that," I said, waving towards the bar, "we have more booze than we can drink in a decade."

Marianna smiled.

"Regarding the cake," she said, "I am thinking of ordering it from this place called 'Sinsations'. I have been told by a few of my friends that their cakes are amazing."

"I have heard of them," said Nysa, "but I hear they are quite expensive."

"Yes, me too," said Marianna, "but everyone tells me that they are unique and exquisite and to die for. Let me talk to them and see how it goes. There are only about two weeks left, and I am not even sure if they have a slot."

She pulled out her phone, and her hands flew across the

screen.

"Here," she said, passing the phone to Nysa, "these are some of Sinsations cakes."

Nysa looked at the photos, swiping slowly.

"Wow," she said, "these look amazing. I wouldn't have the heart to cut any of these!"

"Let's hope they have a slot for us," said Marianna, taking back the phone.

Neither of them thought to show me the photos. Why, I wondered.

"What about the beer and wines?" I asked.

"That's part of the catering," said Marianna, "open bar, including soft drinks and juices."

"Are you planning a theme?" asked Nysa.

I held my breath. No theme, no theme, I prayed. Nysa has made me dress up looking like a fool on more than a few occasions.

"No," said Marianna, glancing at me, and smiling at my relief, "just a regular, fun surprise birthday party."

She took a deep breath.

"I want to share something with you," she said, "but you must keep it absolutely quiet. Not a word to anyone."

Nysa and I looked at one another.

"Okay," said Nysa.

"Promise," I said.

"I feel a little bad talking about this when there has been a death in the firm," she said, "but I am too excited to keep it to myself."

"Enough suspense," said Nysa, her face agog with anticipation.

Marianna smiled a joyous, victorious smile.

"You are talking to the Joint Managing Partner of Nestor & Ross," she said, in a rush of words and a burst of exhilaration.

Nysa jumped up and clapped her hands.

"That is amazing news!" she exclaimed. She stepped forward, bent down and embraced Marianna. "So proud of you, my dear."

It took me a few seconds to react. I was parsing the timeline in my mind.

"Congratulations, Marianna!" I said, also standing up to go and give her a hug. "This is brilliant and well deserved!"

Marianna's smile was Cheshire-like.

"I couldn't believe it when they called me in and told me yesterday," she said, "I felt like I would burst!"

"Oh, this happened yesterday, is it?" I asked.

"Yes, just after lunch," she said, "The Chairperson called me and told me that the Board has decided that I am the best person for the role, and they would be proud if I accepted it."

"Mm-hmm." I said.

"This calls for a celebration!" said Nysa, "Ishmael, would you…"

"No, please no," said Marianna, interrupting her, "I haven't told Shahed yet, and I want to celebrate with all of you on his birthday."

"Ah, that's why you are swearing us to silence," said Nysa.

"Yes, I thought this would be a great birthday present," she said, "what do you think?"

"Oh, absolutely," I said, "it will make his day and his year!"

Nysa agreed with even more enthusiasm.

"Is it okay to feel so happy even if James has just died?" asked Marianna, quieting down a little.

"Those are two unrelated things, aren't they" Nysa said wisely, "yes, we understand you feeling bad about James' passing, but this promotion is something you have worked for over so many years, and it is right that you feel joy and satisfaction!"

With this, we rose and went to the dining room to continue discussing the party over dinner.

Marianna and Nysa spoke about flowers and balloons and canapes. They argued the merits of a live band versus a DJ. They spoke about the dress Marianna was going to buy and which designer she was going to buy it from.

I pitched in from time to time, but my contributions were unnecessary. The rolling stone had budged, and having budged, was picking up momentum at an exhilarating pace.

I finished my dinner.

"May I excuse myself," I asked, "I need to make a call."

I got two impatient glances and an equal number of dismissive nods.

I rinsed my plate in the sink, washed my hands and walked to the balcony.

I pulled out and lit a cigarette.

My career as an assassin seemed not to be going so well so far.

My first target was Greg Closier. The reason for his passing was that he was supposed to be having an affair with Marianna. That was found to be untrue.

The second was Lee Sun Wah. The reason for his passing was that he was at the wrong place at the wrong time and tried to profit from it. Not really a capital offence, you would think.

The third was James Hong. The reason for his being on the hit-list was that he seemed to be hurting Marianna's chances of becoming Managing Partner. Now I find out that she was promoted well before his premature demise.

The smoke swirled around me. There wasn't even a hint of breeze.

The point of being an assassin was to right the wrongs that people committed.

I seemed to be getting the wrongs wrong, and none of the righting right.

Should I stop this? I wondered. Maybe I am not cut out for this profession. Perhaps it needs a more mature, thoughtful, insightful approach, which I seem to be lacking.

I considered the question.

I stubbed out my cigarette.

No, I said to myself. Mistakes happen. My intentions were right. I would deal with Rahul Sinha. There was no doubt about his needing to be terminated. His wrongs were proven and documented. Also, this would be my first 'professional' assignment. Carried out for a third party with no emotional baggage weighing on me. It would be the perfect test run to help me decide whether I should and can transition to assassination as a vocation, as a business.

Then, depending on how I performed, I would decide whether to stop, pause or continue.

I turned to go back in to join the ladies.

Second guessing was for wimps.

INTERLUDE 11

As Ishmael Dollah was having a crisis of conscience while his wife and daughter-in-law were planning a party,

Inspector Julia Binti Shafiq was closing in on her prey.

"See, Chee Wee," she pointed, "look at the photo of the man exiting the restroom."

Chee Wee squinted and looked.

"Now see this," she pointed at her laptop, at a news clipping that said, 'CEO turns around ailing company; returns 4X to shareholders'.

He looked.

"Aren't they the same person?"

Chee Wee wasn't sure.

"They are," said Julia confidently, "I can feel it."

"I am not sure, madam…" started Chee Wee.

"I am!" snapped Julia, "Ishmael Dollah was in the Club. He went into the restroom just after Closier. He came out just before Closier was found murdered. There is no doubt!"

"But, madam," said Chee Wee, "Mr. Closier was poisoned, wasn't he?"

Julia looked at him.

Chee Wee was a great analyst, but he had this terrible habit of bursting her balloon.

"Yes," she said, sourly, "so what? He could have poisoned Closier in the bathroom."

"How?" asked Chee Wee simply.

"How?" snarled Julia, "What do you mean, 'how'?

"If you see the time stamps, madam," Chee Wee said earnestly, "Mr. Dollah, if it was he, was in the restroom for less than four minutes. What poison would be have administered that could have acted so fast and made Mr. Closier collapse and die within four minutes?"

"Also," he continued, "didn't the coroner say that the poison needed at least thirty minutes to act on the nervous system?"

Julia felt a strong emotion pass through her. It was hatred. Of Chee Wee.

Why was he being so unreasonable?

"I don't know!" she said angrily. "If I knew everything, I would be God, wouldn't I?"

Chee Wee wisely refrained from responding.

"I know that Dollah had a hand in this murder," said Julia with conviction, "and I am sure that he also had something to do with Lee's death!"

Chee Wee couldn't let this pass.

"But, madam," he protested, "Mr. Lee's death was ruled by natural causes."

"I don't believe in coincidences, Chee Wee!" exclaimed Julia, "where there is smoke, there is fire!"

"Umm, I am not sure how that adage applies here, madam," ventured Chee Wee.

"Oh, bugger!" said Julia, "I am going to have a cigarette. Just look at the photos again, Chee Wee, and you will see that I am right!"

She stalked out of the conference room.

I am right, she told herself, I know I am.

CHAPTER 36

I opened my eyes on Friday morning.

The usual surge of energy that greeted me was absent.

I continued to lie in bed and stare, unseeingly, at the ceiling.

The question of conscience that I had grappled with on the balcony last night, and that I had thought I had answered firmly, had resurfaced.

Was I an assassin to actually add value? Or was I one because it made me feel of value?

Were my targets deserving of the outcome that I had visited on them? Or were they convenient excuses that would help me feel that I was still relevant?

Was I killing for cause? Or for convenience?

I am and always have been a results-focused, achieve-at-all-costs kind of person. Whether at work, at home, or on the tennis court. Once I have a clear objective, I focus on removing all obstacles in my path to achieving that goal within the timeframe set. Once the bit is in my teeth, I hate the idea of nit-picking and reassessing and hesitating.

Sadly, that is exactly what I was doing now.

And I was depressed.

I did not want to get out of bed.

I did not want to face these uncomfortable questions.

Let me go back to sleep, I thought, and postpone the inevitable.

That was not to be.

"Ishmael, are you awake?"

If there was some way I could have answered 'no' and got away with it, I would have.

I pulled the covers over my head and pretended not to hear.

"Ishmael!"

This was ridiculous. I may not be British, but a man's bed is his castle.

I pulled off the covers.

"What? Why are you waking me up?" I asked, sulkily.

"Sorry, dearest, but there is a courier who insists on handing the package only to you," said Nysa from the door of the bedroom.

"Why?" I asked grumpily, "can you not sign for me?"

"He says no," said Nysa, patiently, "he said he would need to give it to you personally."

I got out of bed, grumbling.

"Could you ask him to wait, please?" I asked.

I went to the bathroom and brushed and washed my face. Then, I reluctantly went to the front door.

"Yes," I asked the young man who was waiting patiently.

"Good morning, sir," he said, "my apologies for troubling you. Mr. Francis has asked me to hand over this envelope to you personally."

"Ah, yes," I said, taking the envelope from him, "thank

you so much."

"My pleasure, sir."

"Have a nice day," I said, and saw him leave.

I took the envelope and went back to the study.

As I crossed the bedroom, I looked longingly inside. However, I was awake now.

I dropped the envelope on my desk.

Then, I changed into my running gear and prepared to meet my thoughts.

When I stepped out of the condo, I realised that it was drizzling steadily. The skies were grey and perfectly matched my mood. And my running shorts.

I turned towards Orchard Road.

Was I on the right track? Or was I just escaping boredom and irrelevance?

Cause or Convenience?

I churned everything that had happened over the past few weeks in my mind.

As I was reviewing, and as I was running, as so very often happens in my mind, reality met rationalization.

You are aware of rationalization, yes?

In psychology, it is defined as a defence mechanism in which people justify difficult or unacceptable feelings with seemingly logical reasons and explanations.

For example, after a divorce, a man may convince himself that his ex-wife wasn't up to his standards or that the separation is a blessing in disguise so he can travel more. So, it wasn't his inadequacy or his inability; it was meant to happen, and for the best.

Rationalization functions to protect the ego from discomfort or distress.

It overrides reality, it circumvents the truth, it cancels what it sees as noise.

Yes, Greg Closier did not have an affair with Marianna. But he was a serial adulterer, betraying both his marriage vows and Jocelyn. Did that not deserve punishment?

Yes, Lee Sun Wah was at the wrong place at the wrong time. But he tried to blackmail me for personal profit. Was that not reprehensible on his part?

Yes, James Hong did not succeed in tearing Marianna down. But he lied about her and possibly about many others, causing distress and hurt. Should he not pay the price?

As I ran and rationalised, the rain dwindled away, the skies gradually brightened to blue, and the sun began to shine.

Perhaps I was a little hasty in my judgement at times, I told myself. But, on the whole I had acted in good faith, with the right intentions, and punished people who had done wrong and who would have continued doing wrong if I had not intervened.

As the burden of doubt gradually dissipated, I found myself running easier and faster.

Of course, I will learn from my mistakes. I am still a novice, and which novice has not made errors, I asked.

The important thing to remember is that Greg Closier's departure has led the way to Marianna becoming Joint Managing Partner. Also, there is no taint on her, which may have continued and spread if Greg had still been alive.

I turned into the last stretch, all uphill, my legs pumping as hard as my heart.

I will do better, I told myself, panting, as I entered our condo and slowed down to a walk.

I would hold myself to higher standards, spend more time and effort on due diligence, and ensure that there was clear value in every assignment I executed.

And now that I was going 'pro', I would be dispassionate. No rose-tinted glasses. No blinkers. I would not depend on hearsay or tattle or my clients' feelings. I would interrogate and evaluate each case on its facts and merits. If my analysis determined that the target genuinely merited termination, I would carry out the assignment. If there was the slightest doubt, I would step back and away.

Also, the world needed someone to clean up its messes. The world needed me to balance the scales. Stopping now would be betraying my reason for being. It would be like a warrior walking away from the battlefield.

I continued walking around the condo, warming down.

I checked my watch – nine kilometres. Not bad for a day that started with me not wanting to get out of bed.

I went into the building and decided I would climb the stairs to our apartment. On the way, I checked my messages and emails.

There was one from Derek.

Let me know when you receive the envelope.

I responded,

Received, thanks.

A minute later, his message was deleted. I followed suit.

Another message from Aziz.

BTW, hope you received the SIMs?

I wrote back,

Yes, received. Sorry that I didn't confirm earlier. Thanks very much.

I had asked Aziz for 2 pre-paid Malaysian SIM cards,

which he had sent along with the package of hazardous material. I had got it and kept it aside but had overlooked acknowledging receipt.

I reached our front door tired but also relieved.

Rationalization had extricated me from so many of my moral dilemmas when I was a CEO. I am glad that it still functioned as well as advertised.

Now to move forward and not be chained by the mistakes of the past.

Time to plan Rahul Sinha's termination.

CHAPTER 37

The surge of energy was back. With me the Force was.

I had a luxurious long shower and joined Nysa for breakfast.

She was quite distracted and kept receiving and sending messages on her phone.

"Is everything okay?" I asked, as I spooned a large portion of yoghurt into my bowl.

"Sorry? Ah, yes, everything's fine," she said, sparing me a moment of her attention, "just chatting with Marianna – there's so much to prepare for Shahed's party, and less than two weeks."

"Is there anything I can do?" I asked, confident in the answer.

"No, not at all," said Nysa, "Marianna and I have everything covered."

"Great!" I said and focussed on breaking my fast.

I finished, helped clear up and went to the study.

I sat at my desk and opened the envelope that Derek had sent me. It contained about ten sheets of paper.

They seemed to be reports and minutes of meetings

relating to the out-placement of the seven employees that Rahul Sinha had caused to leave.

I put my feet up on the settee and read.

Being fired or being encouraged to leave is such a terrible blow. It destroys your self-esteem, makes you question your deepest beliefs about yourself, and shames you in front of your family and friends.

Why me, you think.

Why you, they think.

No reason is enough to explain the insult away.

The company is downsizing, you say. But what about all the employees who continue?

The boss belittled me and abused me. What did you do to deserve that?

The workplace atmosphere was toxic. Why didn't you do something to change it?

A small part of me felt regret. In my career, I had terminated the employment of hundreds of people, even a few thousands. How much ever I may pride myself on the transparent, objective, open approach that I used; how much ever I may take solace from ensuring that I met each and every person individually and personally, explained the situation, did it reduce the pain or wash away the shame?

I had never been on the receiving end. So, I did not truly know.

But I thought not.

The pages from Derek's HR team were written as objectively as possible but reeked of raw emotion.

Of visas cancelled. Of lives disrupted. Of education uprooted.

All this so that one man could feed his ego. These were

not separations because the company needed to stave off disaster. These were people hounded out by unpardonable toxic behaviour.

The familiar rage was building up inside me.

I read each page and then re-read them all.

Individually and together, they were an indictment of Rahul Sinha.

He needed to go.

I put the sheets back into the envelope and slid the envelope in the bottom desk drawer.

I sat back and resumed considering the approaches to this assignment.

Not in his office. Not at his home. Must ideally be accidental.

I turned to the laptop and opened the browser.

'Accidents causing the highest number of fatalities in Singapore', I typed.

I spent the next 20 minutes gleaning through various websites, official and not.

As I digested the statistics and facts and figures, a tiny thought sparked and gradually grew into an ember.

The approach was very different from anything I had thought about or planned so far.

It was based on and depended on the one point that I had listed in our favour when I was analysing the situation previously – that Rahul was ambitious and hungry and would do whatever it took to get to the corner office.

I left the study and walked to the living room balcony.

Lighting a cigarette, I started sketching the outline of the plan.

It would need a lure to attract Rahul.

It would need a meeting to embed the hook.

Once he was on the hook, it would need a road that was relatively camera-free.

I looked at the clustered buildings of the central business district in the distance.

What would the best lure be?

Something that gave him leverage. Something that assured him that he could displace Derek and take his place.

I smoked and thought.

When I stubbed out the cigarette, I had the glimmerings of an idea, but one that would need to be refined substantially.

I went back to the study.

I typed in another request for Google.

After reading the results for a few minutes, I saved some of the information into a separate folder created for Rahul.

Then, another request.

The results to this were very interesting, and to some extent surprising. I saved three pages.

I got up.

I would need to do some driving around.

"Nysa," I called, "I need to go out and complete a couple of chores. Is it okay if I take the car?"

Nysa stepped out of the kitchen.

"Sure, I am not going anywhere now," she said.

"I should be back in a couple of hours," I said, "if I am delayed, please don't wait for me, go ahead and have your lunch."

"Okay," she said, "I'll wait till 1:30 pm for you."

"Great, thanks," I said, and went to collect the car keys. I also printed out the relevant pages that I had saved.

Driving in Singapore is a pleasure. The roads are great, the traffic is usually smooth, barring some places during peak hours, most drivers are courteous and well mannered.

I drove, using the information on the sheets, to specific places.

In each of the three places, I drove slowly, scanning the road on both sides, looking for cameras and paths and people.

All of them seemed to suit my requirements. One of them, however, seemed perfect. I stopped the car on the shoulder and got off. There was nothing next to the road but brush and trees leading down an incline into a rather dense thicket of woods. Almost a forest.

I got in the car and continued driving. The road was unusually bumpy and coarse. I continued straight till I reached a T-junction that connected to a reasonably busy artery.

I took a U-turn and drove back the way I came.

As I neared our condo, more pieces of the plan started fitting into place.

I parked the car, and sat in it for a few minutes, filling in the outlines till most of the plan took clear shape.

It could work, I thought. It could work really well.

I got off from the car and went up to our apartment. It was nearing 1:30 pm.

"Hi Nysa, I am back." I called as I entered.

"Great, I was just going to start," she said as I entered the dining room.

"Thank you for waiting for me," I said, as I washed my

hands in the Utility room and joined her at the table.

"I am glad you are back," she said, "I've been wanting to talk to you. Do you remember my idea of a car for Shahed's birthday?"

I groaned.

CHAPTER 38

"

Hush," said Nysa, "I need your help."

"Yes, dear," I said resignedly, "what is the issue?"

"I shortlisted three cars," she said, "and I narrowed it down the Porsche Taycan."

"What? When?" I sputtered, the mango curry going down the wrong way. "When did you do all this?"

Nysa looked at me smugly.

"Just because you are an engineer and I am not, doesn't mean I am a doofus," she said, archly.

Under no circumstances would I ever call Nysa a doofus. About anything.

But for a person who drove our first car with the handbrake on most of the time, this sudden expertise on cars was a revelation.

"I am a researcher, my dear," she continued, rubbing my nose in it, "I know how to separate fact from fiction."

"Okay, and you narrowed down on the Taycan," I said, "why?"

"Well, for one it's a Porsche, so it's a muscle car," she said, ticking off her fingers, "two, it looks amazing. And three, its electric, so Shahed can continue saving his precious environment."

I was impressed. And dismayed.

"Do you know how much a Taycan costs?" I asked.

"Yes, the model I chose is about four hundred thousand dollars," she said, without flinching.

"Isn't that a lot of money for a car?" I asked, keeping my panic under control.

"Shahed's our only son, Ishmael," said Nysa, using her usual tactic of talking breathily and batting her eyelashes, "and he's such a wonderful boy. So, what if it costs a bit?"

I resisted falling into the trap.

"Four hundred thousand dollars is too much money for a car, Nysa," I said emphatically.

"Anyway," she said, dismissing my words, "that is not the issue here."

"Then what is?" I asked, confused.

"I spoke to the Porsche dealer, and he said that the Taycan has a four-month waiting period," she said, her voice all woebegone.

I manfully prevented a deep sigh of relief.

"Ah, that's such a shame," I said.

"Yes, and you need to find a way around it," said Nysa. Once again with the voice and the eyes.

"How?" I asked, truly flabbergasted.

"I don't know," she shrugged, passing the monkey neatly onto my shoulder, "you are so well connected, with contacts everywhere, I am sure you will find a way."

"I am not even well connected to my mechanic," I protested.

"Ishmael," said Nysa, "you say you love me, can you not

do such a small thing for me?"

From seduction to flattery to blackmail, in three sentences.

"Nysa," I started, "how on earth am I..."

"I have faith in you," she said, "now let's eat, the food is going cold."

Lunch continued, mostly in silence, other than requests to pass this, that or the other, all of which tasted wonderful.

After lunch, I escaped to the study before the subject of cars was brought up again.

No more distractions. I needed to create the bait that would lure Rahul Sinha.

I learnt all about bait when I first joined the marketing department and worked under the Marketing Director, Mr. Kashyap, who was a wonderful boss and mentor.

"What is the best bait to lure a customer?" he asked once, of the team, four of us.

We gave many answers – discounts, promotions, cash rebates, cashbacks, and so on.

He listened and smiled.

"All these are constituents," he said, "but the real bait is self-interest."

He saw the puzzled look on our faces.

"Every human being is wired to protect and preserve and benefit themselves," he said, "it is a genetic condition. And when you present to a human being anything that he believes will contribute to his well-being, his safety, his self-interest, he will be unable to resist it."

"Why do you appreciate flattery even when you know it is not real?" he continued, "because it strokes our ego – self-interest. Why does a woman buy Dove soap? Because it promises her eternal youth and beauty – self-interest."

"Whatever offer you make to your customer, understand the customer and speak to his self-interest, and your product will sell."

Over the years since, I learnt how prescient Mr. Kashyap was.

I learnt how to present products, proposals and ideas always considering and speaking to the self-interest of the buyer, reviewer, or arbiter. When I got it right, success was a foregone conclusion.

I knew what Rahul Sinha wanted.

He wanted Derek Francis gone.

I had to speak to that desire, and make it seem that I could help him achieve his goal.

For that, I would need to do a little creative editing on my laptop.

I fired up the browser and looked for images of Derek. He had been a CEO for eons, and there were photos of him galore. Derek speaking at conferences, handing out awards, receiving awards, cutting ribbons – there seemed no end.

I chose five photos of Derek in positions that would best suit my needs.

I opened a new window and looked for photos of senior managers from two of Jetsmart's largest vendors – Wartsila and Daikin. I found enough in similar situations – giving or getting some kind of award, looking modest and proud. I saved four of these.

Then, I opened an application called Photopea. This is not as well-known as its cousin, Photoshop, but is an amazing tool.

I spent the next two hours creating a new reality, a reality that I believed would be the bait that Rahul would not be able to resist.

I collaged three new photos from the nine that I had saved.

One of them showed Derek in a rather shady room, receiving a packed envelope from the South Asia Regional Head of Wartsila. Two of them showed Derek in different locations, receiving a packed envelope from Daikin's VP - Marketing.

The photos were appropriately a little grainy and slightly blurred, as if they had been taken from a distance, but there was no missing Derek or his companions. And it was clear in each photo that something was changing hands.

The next part was a little more challenging.

I created a watermark. The watermark read,

SGPI Private Investigations | +65 5555 4444

Then, I set about printing the photos with the watermark repeated in a staggered manner on the reverse.

It took me a few tries to get it right.

The final products were very convincing, even though I thought so myself.

I printed two of each.

I stashed away the digital files in the appropriate password-protected folder.

I deleted the browser cache.

Then, I picked up the phone and called Mr. Joseph Wing of SGPI.

Many years ago, I needed the services of a private investigator. I won't tell you why, just now. A friend recommended SGPI and told me to specifically ask for Joseph Wing.

I did, and from that initial transaction, a close relationship developed.

I used SGPI and Joseph's services quite a few times in the ensuing years.

I recommended Joseph to others, and he was grateful. He was even more grateful when I put SGPI on retainer with the company I was running at the time. But he was most grateful when I gave his son a job in the company and helped him build his career,

"Hi, Mr. Dollah," said Joseph, picking up on the first ring.

"Hello, Joseph, how have you been?" I asked. "And how is the family, especially young Brad?"

We spoke for a couple of minutes, catching up on the more than two years since we had last met. He told me how Brad had been promoted and was now running his own department. I congratulated him.

Then, I explained the favour that I needed.

"Mr. Dollah," said Joseph, "absolutely no problem. I'll take care of it, don't worry."

I knew from experience that when Joseph said, 'don't worry', I did not have to worry.

"Thank you, Joseph," I said, as we came to the end of the call, "I hope to catch up for a drink sometime."

I shut the phone.

The planets were lining up well.

INTERLUDE 12

As Ishmael Dollah was manufacturing bait to lure Rahul Sinha while simultaneously avoiding discussing cars with Nysa,

Inspector Julia Binti Shafiq was being dressed down by her boss.

"But, sir…" she started.

He held up his hand.

"This is the third time we are speaking about this, Inspector," he said.

Deputy Director Ang Eng Leong sat behind a large desk. His chair was ergonomic and stain free. His office had a window overlooking the park next to the CID headquarters.

His normally smiling face was forbidding and severe.

"Sir, may I please explain," requested Julia, who was sitting in a comfortable chair across the Deputy Director, "I believe we have established a connection between Mr. Closier's killing and Mr. Lee's death. We now need to…"

"Inspector," the Deputy Director interrupted, "I believe Mr. Lee's death was ruled by natural causes?"

"Yes, sir, but that may not be the case," said Julia.

"What proof do you have that the death was suspicious?"

"Um, none yet, sir, but…"

"Okay, what is the connection between the two deaths?"

"There was a man present in the restroom when Mr. Closier died. Mr. Lee was also there just before that. I believe…" Julia was interrupted again.

"But Mr Closier died of poisoning, I thought?"

"Yes, sir, but there is more to his death than that," said Julia. She stopped.

"And what is it that you have?" asked the Deputy Director.

"Mr. Closier worked in a law firm where the daughter-in-law of the man who was in the restroom also worked…" Julia tapered off.

Even she could hear how fragile her argument was.

"Inspector," said the Deputy Director, "it is okay to have doubts. It is fine to dig deeper. But it is important that we do not get obsessed with one case or one suspect. That is the path to failure and condemnation."

"Yes, sir," muttered Julia.

"Your case load has backed up quite a bit," he continued, "please go ahead and clear it, and in the meantime if any evidence surfaces on the Closier killing, please feel free to bring it to me."

"Yes, sir," said Julia, standing.

"Thank you, Inspector, and all the best," said the Deputy Director, standing and smiling.

"Good evening, sir," said Julia as she left the office and closed the door gently behind her.

The first thing she noticed was Chee Wee. He was standing in the corridor, moving from foot to foot as if he needed to urinate desperately.

He rushed forward as soon as he saw her emerge.

"Madam, just got this despatch from Ang Mo Kio Police," he said, handing over a sheet of paper to Julia.

Julia took it and read it, first quickly and then a little slower.

She looked up at Chee Wee, eyes blazing.

"Nestor & Ross again! This is Dollah's work!" she hissed.

Chee Wee was impressed. Not many people could hiss a 'd' or a 'w'.

"Madam, isn't it best that we talk to the Investigating Officer before taking any action?" he asked, pausing after 'any' to indicate his diplomatic avoidance of the word 'hasty'.

Julia's eyes flared, as she kept her stare on Chee Wee. He looked right back without blinking.

She took a deep breath. She nodded.

"Yes, you are right, Chee Wee," she said, "let's do that."

CHAPTER 39

I sent a WhatsApp message to Derek.

"Could you send me Rahul's mobile number?"

Thirty seconds later, I received his response.

"+65 7744 3322"

I deleted my message.

Five minutes later, he had deleted his.

I looked for and found my Oppo phone. It still had 30% charge, even though I had neglected its well-being.

I put in one of the Malaysian SIM cards into the phone.

I looked at the time. 6:40 pm.

Time for a walk.

I changed into my running gear, picked up the Oppo phone and went to the living room. Nysa was reading a thick tome. She seemed completely engrossed.

"Nysa, my dear," I said, gently, "I am going for a short walk. Will be back by 7:30 pm, okay?"

She looked up. Her eyes were moist as if she had been crying. In one hand, she held a bundle of crumpled tissues.

"Okay," she said, her voice unsteady.

As a caring husband, you would have expected that I

should have stayed, asked what the problem was, and then been there for support and encouragement.

I agree. Been there, tried that.

Nysa loves to read. More importantly, she loves to read tragic and mostly historic tales of war and murder and destitution and pillage. Then, she cries and feels terrible for long lost people who suffered, struggled and died pitiable deaths.

There is nothing I can do.

The crimes were committed centuries ago. The people who died have been reborn thirty, maybe forty times.

So, I look sympathetic and find somewhere else to be asap.

Which is what I did now.

As soon as Nysa said okay, I turned and jogged to the front door and thence to the elevator.

Ten minutes later, I was walking down Clemenceau Avenue, inhaling the wonderful aromas from Newton Food Court.

As I passed Winstedt, the road became quieter, with almost no one on the footpaths.

I stopped. I sent a message with an attachment. Then, I dialled Rahul Sinha's number.

"Hello?" he said, obviously not recognising the number.

"Mr. Sinha, I have just sent a photo to your phone by WhatsApp," I said, "please see it and then decide if you want to continue this call."

There was silence on the line for twenty seconds.

"What is this? Who is this?" he asked, but his voice was calm. He was a cool customer.

"I know that you want to be CEO of Jetsmart," I said, "I

have the means to help you achieve that dream now rather than wait for a few years for the current CEO to retire."

"Who is this?" Rahul asked again. "I cannot comment on anything you have said without knowing who you are and what this is about."

"Smart man," I said, "I will cut to the chase. We have photos that will compel the Board to dismiss Mr. Francis. Would you like to buy them?"

He was stumped for a moment.

"You don't have to say yes or no now," I said. "I am going to be at the Rifle Range Nature Park tomorrow at 6:30 pm. If you are interested, come and meet me. I will be wearing a pair of blue jeans, a black full-sleeved t-shirt and a red baseball cap."

"To do what?" he asked. Very non-committal. Smart.

"I will show you three physical photos and their provenance," I said, "if you like them and want the whole set, we will discuss and agree on a price. Then, you will be taken to see the whole set to confirm that it is not a con. Finally, you will pay us, and we will hand over all the photos to you, to do what you want."

"I am not free tomorrow evening…" he started to say.

"I am sorry," I said, cutting him off, "this is a one-time offer. It expires tomorrow at 6:45 pm. Have a good day."

"Wait…" he started, but I closed the call. I removed the SIM card, broke it into two and threw the pieces into the nearest bin.

Then, I walked home.

This is the riskiest ploy so far, I thought. It was exciting. Will he or won't he?

The next thought that struck me was that I did not have a black full-sleeved t-shirt and a red baseball cap.

I had to go back to our apartment, pick up my wallet and then go to Orchard Road.

Better to have dinner first.

I returned to the apartment and cautiously looked for Nysa.

She was not in her usual position on the sofa.

"Hi Nysa?" I called.

"Hey Ishmael," she called back from the vicinity of the dining room. He voice was back to normal, all melody and sunshine.

I heaved a sigh and went to the dining room.

Nysa was laying the final touches to the dining table. I kissed her and sat down.

Dinner was a substantive spread.

"Wow, this is a lot!" I exclaimed.

"Yes, Siti and I have been trying out some recipes for Shahed's birthday lunch," said Nysa. "Look, here is the Gado-Gado because Shahed loves vegetables. And here is the vegetable Sayur Asem, a tangy soup."

"Both of them look amazing," I said.

"Tell me how they taste, and which one would Shahed like?" said Nysa.

"I will do the former, but you will have to ask Marianna about Shahed's current tastes," I said, "all I can remember is chocolate ice cream and Reese's peanut butter cups."

She laughed.

"That was when he was a young boy," she said.

"Those were his two main food groups till he finished

college," I retorted.

I dug into all the dishes, familiar and new.

As always, Nysa's cooking had no pareil.

"Nysa," I said, seriously, "I am running out of superlatives to use for your food. I will need to learn new languages to find new words."

Nysa smiled.

"Thank you, Ishmael," she said, "and which of the two dishes do you like more?"

I paused and considered.

"The Gado-Gado, I think, but by a very slim margin," I said.

We finished dinner and cleared up. If I had to buy the clothes I needed, I would have to rush.

"Nysa," I said, as I wiped my hands dry. "I need to buy cigarettes, be back in a few minutes."

"Bye," she said, "I'll be finishing my book."

I moved quickly and walked-ran to OGs on Orchard Road. I had heard that they were shutting down, which was such a shame.

The store was open.

I went in, picked up a black full-sleeved t-shirt, size M, reconsidered, picked up two, and then went in search of a red baseball cap. I found one, though it was more maroon than red. Can't be helped, I thought, as I stood in the queue at the cashier's counter. I had a sudden thought and went back into the store. I found a pair of cheap sunglasses that fit me and went back to the cashier.

I reached our apartment and went directly to the Utility room and put the three articles of clothing in the washing machine and switched it on.

"What are you washing, Ishmael?" called Nysa.
"Oh nothing," I lied, "just my sweat soaked clothes."
"Oh, okay, sweetie."
Was I a really good liar or was Nysa more gullible than most?

CHAPTER 40

Saturday morning began with a frisson of excitement and two hours of back-against-the-wall tennis.

I showered in the Club, changed and drove again to the road and spot that I deemed most optimal for this evening. I did not stop, just slowed down and looked carefully for cameras or any public works that may capture or interrupt the actions I had planned.

Then, I drove home for a much-deserved breakfast.

"Darling," said Nysa, as we were eating, "I will be meeting Marianna at 11:00 and going shopping with her. I hope that's okay?"

No, that was not okay. I needed our car. Nysa and Marianna shopping meant that the car would be gone till the last shop in Singapore closed.

"Ah, are you picking her up?" I asked.

"No, we are taking Marianna's car," said Nysa, much to my relief.

"Okay, have a wonderful day together!" I said, "and please don't buy any cars."

"Ishmael!" growled Nysa, in mock-anger.

Smiling, I washed up and retired to my study and started putting together everything I needed for the evening.

The photos, in a plain envelope.

Mask, gloves, sunglasses.

Jeans, black t-shirt, cap.

Marlin spike.

A couple of damp rags in a plastic bag.

The Oppo phone with the second Malaysian SIM card.

An old pair of running shoes, which were on the verge of being discarded.

I sat in my chair, turned to the bay window, looked out and reviewed the plan again. And again.

There were risks, but I could see no other way of executing this assignment. Fortune favours the bold and the prepared, I said to myself.

At 11:15, Nysa came into the study to say bye. I kissed her hard.

"I don't know why, but I like it," she smiled, winked, and left.

The afternoon sped like molasses.

Would Rahul come? Has he taken the bait? Would he have informed anyone?

I ate a lonely lunch, ameliorated by watching 'The Martian' on Netflix.

I put away the food, washed the dishes, wiped the table.

I completed the NYT crossword.

Would Rahul follow the script? Or would he produce his own?

Finally, I picked up my iPad and began reading the latest

issue of the Economist.

Whenever you are feeling down or worried or depressed, read the Economist. Its pages are suffused with so much gloom and fear, that the problems you are facing almost seem like blessings. The magazine starts with a post-mortem and ends in an obituary.

By 5:00 pm, I was feeling so much better. The travails of a divided USA, the meltdown of the British leadership, the coups, the famines, the floods, the frauds, the inflation, the pandemic – God, what was I worrying about? I just had to terminate one employee.

I arose with a spring in my step.

Time to go.

I wore what I told Rahul I would be wearing, taped the marlin spike to my left forearm with the mobile armband, collected everything I needed and left the apartment.

I was in Rifle Range Nature Park by 5:45 pm. I had parked the car about 800 metres away, in a low-end mall. I walked down the trail. There were a few people walking and even fewer running, but as the sky darkened, the park gradually emptied.

I walked back to near the entrance. I placed the envelope, the Oppo phone and the marlin spike under a bush. Then, I leaned against a light pole and waited. If Rahul brought the authorities along, I had nothing on me that would incriminate me.

I could see the carpark from where I was standing. There were only three cars left, and one of them was preparing to drive away.

I looked at my watch. 6:35 pm. My bait didn't seem to have worked. I would give it ten minutes more and then leave. Frustrating, but that is the way things turn out, sometimes.

6:40 pm.

I straightened out, ready to start walking to the exit, when I saw a car pull into the carpark.

It was past dusk, and I was wearing sunglasses, so I could not see whether it was Rahul. The driver got out, locked the car and walked towards where I was standing. When he was about fifty metres away, he walked under a streetlight.

It was Rahul.

I waited.

He came closer, squinting. The yellowish light was insufficient for him to make out the red cap.

"Hi, Mr. Sinha," I said.

He started. And stopped.

"Who are you?" he asked, loudly.

I did not reply.

I walked to the bush, picked up the items I had parked there. I pushed the marlin spike, butt down, into my back pocket, and the phone into my front pocket. I held the envelope in my hand and walked to him.

"Here, take a look," I said.

He took the envelope warily from my hand. He opened the flap and pulled out the three photos. He stepped closer to the light and peered at the photos. When he looked up, his eyes were gleaming.

"How do I know that these are not..." he began.

"Look at the backs," I said.

Rahul turned the photos around and saw the watermarks.

"You can call them right now and confirm that these have been taken by them. Ask for Joseph Wing," I said.

"Uh, it's okay," he started to say.

"No, I insist," I said, "without provenance, these photos

are useless."

Rahul pulled out his phone, and dialled SGPI's number. He got an operator, it seemed, because he asked to be connected with Joseph Wing.

He switched on the speakerphone.

"Yes," said Joseph.

"Mr. Wing," said Rahul, "I have a couple of photos with your watermark on the back. I was told that these are your work."

"Uh-uh. What photos are these?" asked Joseph.

"Photos of Derek Francis of Jetsmart," said Rahul.

"What!" Joseph's voice rose sharply. "How do you have these photos? Who are you? These are private and confidential!"

Rahul cut off the call. He looked at me.

"Okay, but these are unclear pictures and don't really prove very much," he said.

"I have about twenty more, each one more damning than the other," I said. "I showed you ones that can be explained away. The remaining cannot."

"This is not just about accepting bribes. Your CEO is having an affair with the young and beautiful wife of your independent Director, Mr. Webb. I have that, too."

That was the tipping point when greed overtook reason in Rahul's mind.

"Where are they?" he asked, "I must see them."

"Absolutely," I said, "I will take you to them right away. Once you are satisfied, we will discuss price, payment and delivery."

"Yes, let's go!" his voice was urgent. "Do you have a car? Should I follow you?"

"No, I don't drive," I said, "I will come with you in your car. I will tell you where to go."

A sliver of reason beckoned at Rahul.

He dismissed it. He put the photos back in the envelope and pulled out his key fob.

"Okay, come on," he said, sealing his fate.

CHAPTER 41

We walked to his car. By now, it was the only one in the carpark.

He clicked the car open and got in. I went to the other side and got in in the back.

He turned around.

"What are you doing?" he asked, surprised.

"I don't drive because I get car sick in the front," I said. "I only take cabs."

He looked at me, frowning. I buckled my seatbelt,

"Let's go," I said.

He turned back, put his seatbelt on, started the car and began driving.

I sat back, trying to look as unthreatening as possible. I gave him crisp directions, informing him well before any turns.

Soon, we were on the road that I had mapped.

"Where are we going?" he asked, his voice annoyed.

"Another few minutes," I said.

I carefully unclasped the seatbelt.

I moved gradually to the right and pulled out the marlin

spike. Five hundred metres before the spot I had marked, I slid to the right, leaned forward and placed the marlin spike against his neck, roughly at the point of his jugular.

"What!" he shouted, and the car swerved.

"Relax," I said, pressing the tip till it made a mark in his neck, "this is just a precaution. Slow down and move to the left."

Rahul had never encountered a life-threatening situation in his life. He was clearly terrified. His eyes were wide open and switching between the windshield and the rear-view mirror. His breath was hitching, in gasps. He obeyed my instructions.

As we reached the exact point, I said, "Slow down further and turn off the road."

He slowed and gradually came onto the shoulder.

"Further left," I said, "Now!"

"My car will get scratched," he wailed.

"Now!" I repeated.

He turned the wheel into the brush.

As he did, I placed the marlin spike between my teeth, and leaning further forward, took his head in both my hands. I wrenched it to the left.

I am sure you have seen movies where the hero comes across the bad guy, and after about 45 seconds of improbable brawling, takes the bad guy's head and twists it sharply, ending the brawl and the bad guy.

It always seems so simple.

Rahul's neck did not cooperate. Either it was made of much hardier stuff than the normal bad guy, or there was something to the technique that I had failed to grasp.

His head twisted but stayed firm on his shoulders.

"Heeeey!" he cried, "what the hell…"

I tried again and twisted his head sharply to the right.

By now, the car had come to a halt, about twenty metres from the road, within the trees.

Rahul started scrabbling at his seatbelt. I had no time to lose.

I held his head with all my strength and pushed it hard forward.

Bingo! His head hit the steering wheel with a meaty thud. His body went loose. I pulled him back. I put my hands again at his jaw and crown and twisted with all my strength.

The car resounded with a crack, and Rahul's head flopped loose.

I pushed his body forward and it fell, with his head resting on the steering wheel.

I was exhausted and panting. I still had the marlin spike between my teeth. I took it out and held it in my hand. I was glad that I didn't have to resort to Plan B, which was to insert the spike into Rahul's ear and scramble his brains. There is no way a capable coroner would have missed it in this situation.

I sat back in the seat and took a couple of minutes to recover.

When my breathing returned to normal, I got out of the right-side door. I kept the door open. I pushed the spike into my back pocket. I pulled out the plastic bag with the rags. I took out one and wiped the seat, the back of Rahul's seat, the headrest and every other spot I could have plausibly leaned any part of myself that was not clothed or gloved.

I put the rag in my pocket and removed another one and repeated the exercise. This time I wiped the entire back seat as well as the passenger seat.

I put both the rags into the plastic bag and pushed them into my pocket.

Then, I opened the front driver's side door.

I switched on the phone light and examined Rahul to see if there were any marks left by my hands. Nothing on the right.

I carefully pulled him back and removed the top part of the seatbelt from across his body and allowed it to snap back behind him. Now it seemed like he had only the waist belt on.

I went over to the passenger side, opened the door, and knelt on the seat and examined Rahul's left. Nothing as far as I could see.

I stepped out and closed all the doors.

I walked about five metres away.

The car was facing downward on an incline, its bonnet against a tree trunk. The bonnet was only lightly damaged.

There were some scratches on the sides and the bonnet.

Would forensics accept this scene as a fatal accident? I didn't know. But this was the best I could do.

I turned to go.

The photos! I remembered. God, what was I thinking!

I went back and opened the driver side door. I probed and pushed and gradually pulled out the envelope containing the photos. I put it into my pocket along with the phone. I shut the door.

I stood for two minutes. Was there anything else I had forgotten?

Nothing came to mind.

I needed to leave before my luck ran out and a nosy car

came by and stopped.

I turned and started walking. I walked about ten metres away from the road. It was painful, with dips and rises and sudden bursts of roots, and I stumbled many times in the dark. After about twenty minutes, I came to a small beaten path, which led to a fence and then ran parallel to the fence. About two hundred metres later, it came out into a small meadow, one of those incongruous patches of green that dot Singapore arbitrarily.

I walked through the meadow in the dark and came to a narrow road that led to a park that led to a two-lane road that eventually led, after four kilometres, to the mall where I had parked my car.

I pulled off my sunglasses and gloves. I dropped them into a bin near a passing bus stop. I dropped the plastic bags containing the rags into another bin. I dropped the cap into a third bin, just outside a streetside restaurant. I covered the bit of marlin spike showing above my back pocket with my t-shirt.

As I entered the mall, I checked myself in the silvered glass doors. I saw an unremarkable old man, cautiously masked, dressed in jeans, t-shirt and walking shoes, coming for his car after a walk.

I drove to the condo, parked, switched off the engine and sat in the silence.

I had executed my fourth assignment.

After about five minutes, I got out, went up to our apartment, took off my mask, clothes, socks and shoes and put them into a plastic bag.

Nysa wasn't back yet.

Then, I had a scalding shower, washing away much more than the sweat and stain.

I changed into my running gear, picked up the bag with the clothes and shoes, and walked to the nearest food court, where I went to the disposal area and distributed the articles singly in seven different bins full of food waste. These would be cleared by the morning.

Then I walked back home.

I didn't feel like having dinner. I changed into my night clothes and went into the bedroom. I lay down and opened my iPad and started reading.

I was asleep before I knew it.

INTERLUDE 13

As Ishmael Dollah was standing under the streetlight, waiting for Rahul Sinha to enter his deadly web,

Inspector Julia Binti Shafiq was having one of the worst days of her life.

About half hour ago, she had got a call from the public prosecutor's office. It was her friend, Vera Chen.

"…and the lawyer claimed that Madame Soon was mentally unstable, and that the son, Boon Tay, was on the spectrum," Vera had said, "also, they brought a letter from the local MP pleading for clemency…"

"And?" asked Julia, grinding her teeth.

"So, the judge referred them for mental evaluation," said Vera, "and released them on bail on the husband's recognizance. I am so sorry, Julia, but you know how it is."

"What do you think will be the outcome, Vera?" asked Julia, clutching for straws.

"I am not going to sugar coat it, Julia," said Vera, "no previous convictions or arrests, which means counselling, maybe a couple of weeks in jail, up to a month, perhaps? The son will be seen as a minor and walk away altogether."

After the call, Julia had sat at her desk, rubbing her forehead with her thumbs. She had a terrible headache.

How can this happen, she wondered? That, too, in a country like Singapore, which holds itself to such high standards.

How can they let two murderers go free?

But this was not the only cause of Julia's dismay and headache.

The whole day was a disaster.

"No, Inspector," the Investigating Officer from Ang Mo Kio who was the officer-in-charge of James Hong's case had said, "we went through the apartment with a fine-tooth comb. There was nothing that indicated foul play."

"But," Julia had sputtered, "how could a young man…"

"Hong was drinking some really potent whisky, almost eighty percent alcohol," the IO had continued, "and he was doing this in the bath. He seemed to have passed out and slid into the water. The coroner found a high alcohol content in his blood and water in his lungs."

"Has the body been tested for toxic substances?" Julia had asked, at her wit's end. "Any suspicious camera feeds?"

"I don't know about the tests for poisons," the IO had replied, "but we checked all the feeds we could, which were very few and far between, and nothing much really…"

Julia had thanked the IO with very poor grace.

She had nothing concrete with which to go after Dollah.

Julia knew it was him, knew that he was responsible somehow for the deaths of Closier and Lee and Hong, but she had no shred of evidence.

As her head throbbed, she felt an unusual emotion.

Respect.

The man is a bastard, but he is a cunning, careful bastard, she thought. A cold, calculating son of a bitch.

She looked for her bag, pulled it to her, rummaged and extracted a bottle of Panadol. She opened it and dry swallowed four.

Dollah must pay.

As must Madam Soon and that delinquent son of hers.

She sat back.

Her mind started evaluating options that she had never dreamt of considering ever before.

CHAPTER 42

I woke early on Sunday and practically jumped out of bed.

Nysa was still asleep next to me, snoring softly.

I brushed, washed, wore my running gear, drank two glasses of water and set out for my run. The dawn was still half hour away, and the streets were silent and cool.

I ran towards the river, planning to head for the Gardens By The Bay. My footsteps echoed in the gloom.

Yesterday was successful. My first professional assassination. I felt a sense of muted pride. It was muted because I knew that my success was as much due to luck and timing as it was due to planning and execution.

To continue in this profession, I needed to ramp up my resources. Better information, smarter tools, back up plans, some much needed training. Yes, my preparation was as good as it could be, but without the appropriate resources, all the preparation in the world could still end in abysmal failure.

I needed a team.

And I had no idea where to get one. Or how.

I turned onto the riverside boardwalk. The restaurants

were closed. The river exuded calm.

I cleared my mind of all thoughts.

Let me enjoy the run, I thought.

The Gardens By The Bay were stunning at sunrise. I felt regret as I left them to return. My run back became increasingly warmer as the sun rose and chased me to our condo.

When I walked into the apartment at 7:15 AM, the quiet told me that both Nysa and Siti were enjoying their Sunday morning in bed.

I showered as quietly as I could.

Then, I took my phone and went to the balcony. I hadn't seen my phone since 5:00 pm or so yesterday. I thumbed through the various messages and texts and emails.

Only one caught my eye.

It was from Joseph Wing, received last night,

Hope everything went well?

I replied,

Good morning, Joseph. Yes, perfectly.

It seemed he was awake, too,

Great. Glad to be of help.

I replied.

Thank you, my friend.

I went against everything that I believed in and sent him a thumbs up emoji.

Within a minute he had deleted all his messages.

Within thirty seconds after that, I deleted mine.

I kept the phone down and lit a cigarette.

I gazed out at Singapore, my mind as calm as the cityscape before me.

I had one more task to carry out.

Nysa wanted to buy a Porsche Taycan for Shahed.

I finished my cigarette and got busy on the phone.

Hi Derek, good morning.

I need a little help.

Jetsmart was one of Singapore's largest importers and third-party stockists of spares and consumables for a wide range of industries including automobiles. Derek would know all the car dealers in Singapore.

Two minutes later,

Hi Ishmael, good morning.

What can I do for you?

I took a little while framing Nysa's issue. Then, I said,

Can you help with the Porsche dealer? I believe they are known as Prime Auto or something.

He replied within seconds,

I had a game of golf with the MD of Prime Auto yesterday. Let me see what I can do.

I did it again. I sent Derek a thumbs up emoji.

Two in one day. I was going native.

As I stepped back in from the balcony, I hear Siti in the kitchen.

I wished her a good morning and expressed my desperate need for sustenance.

She laughed.

"Two minutes, sir," she said.

As I ate and read the newspaper, my mind continued churning.

How and from where was I going to get a team?

The yoghurt with Nysa's famous cranberry sauce almost drove that thought from my mind. Almost.

The team needed at least three members – one with connects into law enforcement, one with the ability to access non-public information and one who could handle logistics and resources.

For the moment, I was at a loss. I didn't even know where to start looking.

And if I wasn't able to put together a team, I may have to reconsider my new profession. I hated the idea of doing that. Especially just after my first victorious assignment.

I parked the problem in my mental 'pending issues' folder and continued to read about floods and famines and war.

After breakfast, I went to the study.

I sat at my laptop and erased everything that I had saved on the Rahul Sinha assignment.

I checked the recycle bin and the browser caches. All clear.

I hear Nysa waking up and heard her speaking to Siti. I then heard her footsteps coming toward the study.

"Good morning, sweetheart," I said.

"Good morning," she smiled, as she sipped from her mug of tea, "you were fast asleep by the time I returned. Tired?"

"Yes, a little," I replied. "How was your day?"

"Oh, brilliant," said Nysa, "Marianna and I had a wonderful time!"

She sat on the settee.

"We found some amazing…" her phone rang.

"Just a minute, Ishmael," she said, looking at the screen. She accepted the call.

"Hello?" she said.

"Yes, this is she."

"Oh, good morning, yes, this is a good time, please go ahead."

Her eyes widened.

"Wow, that's great! Thank you!"

"Can I come today? Around 1:30 pm? Perfect, I will see you then, thank you!"

She looked at me with delight.

"Guess who that was!" she asked, and proceeded not to wait for my response, "It was Prime Auto! It seems they have a Taycan available! What luck!"

"That is great news," I said, "though I still think…"

"Oh pish, Ishmael," Nysa said, as she stood up, "this is manifest destiny! It was meant to happen."

"I need to shower and call Marianna to see if she can come with me," she said, "I'll talk to you later."

When she reached the door of the study, she paused and looked back.

"Did you have anything to do with this?" she asked.

"Me?" replied, "No, nothing. I don't even want you to buy the car."

She smiled tentatively, unconvinced.

Then she turned and left.

I smiled and picked up my phone to check if I had any new messages.

I did.

Mr. Dollah, this is Inspector Julia Binti Shafiq of the CID. Could you call me when you are free?

I did.

CHAPTER 43

It was 2:00 pm.

Nysa had left with Marianna for the Prime Auto showroom.

I sat at a table in the corner of the Orchard Central food court. I had a glass of soursop juice in front of me. I knew that I was supposed to feel tense, but I didn't. I was curious, yes, but less worried than I should have been.

I saw a young lady walk towards me. She was beautiful. About five and a half feet tall, with skin as smooth as silk and as warm as caramel. She was dressed in a pair of jeans and a t-shirt, and they hugged her toned body willingly. Her bearing exuded confidence, as if she owned the place.

I stood up.

"Mr. Dollah?" she said, in a husky voice.

"Yes," I replied.

She pulled the chair opposite me and sat down. I followed suit.

"How can I help you, Inspector?" I asked. "And can I get you something to drink?"

She looked at me, her deep brown eyes mesmerising.

"I know all about you, Mr. Dollah," she said.

I sat back in the uncomfortable chair.

"Mm-hmm," I said.

"I know about Closier and Lee and Hong. I know that you are responsible." she continued.

"I am so sorry, what is this about?" I asked, feigning ignorance. And bafflement.

She ignored me.

"You are a cold-blooded murderer, Mr. Dollah," stated Julia bluntly, "and I will prove it."

"I am so sorry," I said again, expressionless. The meeting was getting interesting. "I don't understand these accusations. Should I hire a lawyer, or…"

"If I were to accuse you formally, I would be doing that in a much less pleasant ambience," said Julia, her tone turning cold, "this is not an accusation. It is a statement of facts that both of us know are true."

"I am at a loss," I said, trying to sound as regretful as possible, "perhaps you are mistaking me for someone else?"

"Mr. Dollah, let's dispense with the pretence, okay," said Julia, "I don't have the time or patience, and I suspect you are a busy man, too."

"Okay," I said, beginning to enjoy myself, "Please go ahead and say what you have to say. I am here already. I may as well hear you out."

"Good," she said, "I know that you are the one who was responsible for the deaths of Greg Closier, Lee Sun Wah and James Hong. I know it, but I don't have enough proof. Given time, I will get it, and then you are going to prison for life, Mr. Dollah, if not to the execution chamber."

"I hear you," I said, working hard to keep my face from breaking into a triumphant smile. Welcome to my parlour,

Julia, as the spider said to the fly.

"I have come here to discuss an alternate proposal," said Julia. I could see her confidence wavering a little. "I am not comfortable with this, but I believe it is necessary."

"Yes?" I asked, with genuine interest.

"There are some criminals who are not paying for their crimes," she said, "and I want you to ensure that they are punished."

Now the meeting became really, really interesting.

"Mm-hmm." I said.

"There are two people that I want you to deal with now," said Julia. "If you do that, I will step back from other investigations." She looked into my eyes. Her eyes were gorgeous. I couldn't look away.

"And who are these two people?" I asked with an effort to keep the conversation on track.

"A mother and son who tortured and murdered their helper," she said, her voice cracking a little. She reached into her pocket and pulled out a slip of paper. She slid it across the table.

"And they are not being punished by the law because…" I prompted, as I picked up the slip.

"The system is flawed," she said, defensively, "and some categories of murders are seen as less heinous than others."

"I understand," I said, "Julia, if I may…"

"You will address me as Inspector," she interrupted, her voice brooking no dissent.

"Very well. Inspector, I am not sure how I can help, but may I consider what you have said and come back to you?" I said, "also, there are some questions that arise, which I may need to collate and obtain detailed responses to."

"I am not giving you a choice here, Mr. Dollah," said Julia, "you will do as I ask, or you will suffer the consequences."

Julia had evidently been seeing movies with menacing Russian villains.

"I hear you, Inspector," I said, keeping my tone bland, "perhaps we can plan a follow-on meeting in a couple of days?"

She took a deep breath. Her face looked uncompromising. And regal.

"Okay," she said, "two days, no more."

She rose. As did I.

I put out my hand to shake. Julia looked at it with disdain.

"You and I are not friends. Or partners. Or anything," she said, coldly. "You are a necessary evil, Mr. Dollah, with the emphasis on evil."

She turned and walked away. She looked as good leaving as she did arriving.

I sat down again. I let my smile, suppressed for too long, break out. It felt good.

Two emotions contributed to the smile.

The first was an overwhelming sense of relief.

The police did not have any evidence that could incriminate me. They may have suspicions, but no proof. Also, based on what I had heard, Julia had no clue about Rahul Sinha. Yes, it was less than 24 hours, but still. If she had had the slightest suspicion, she would have had no hesitation in adding him to her list of my victims.

The second was a fierce sense of elation.

Julia, whether she knew it or not, had become the first member of the team I wanted to build. I had been wondering where to look; instead, she came looking for me.

I didn't know whether it was the law of attraction or the law of awareness that worked, and I didn't care. My team had begun to take form.

And my first team member was drop-dead gorgeous. It was by no means a necessary condition, but so much better than an overweight, hairy man with body odour, don't you think?

Finally, the fact that Julia was in the CID was a dream come true. She would have access to information that a regular police officer would not normally have.

I took a sip of my juice. It was cool and tart. Appropriate, I thought.

It occurred to me that while Julia might be an excellent investigator, she was a terrible negotiator. She showed me her hand too soon. And it was a losing hand. Julia may have thought that she was going to coerce me into doing her bidding. But she had nothing to coerce me with. No evidence, no testimony, no corroboration. So, when I did what she asked me to, I would be luring her into my world. Each step she took towards me would enmesh her. Each meeting she had with me would snare her. Every assignment I completed would bind her.

My smile grew wider as I evaluated the possibilities.

I opened the slip of paper that Julia had passed on to me.

It contained two names and an address. The mother and the son, I believe.

I found it both curious and amusing that every time I completed one assignment, another was brought to my attention. It was almost as if fate was decreeing that it needed me to keep executing these assignments on its behalf.

I vaguely recalled the names. I remembered reading a

small news item about a family collaborating to abusing a helper till she died.

Julia had found two very deserving targets.

I gulped down my juice and walked to the tray return area and dropped the plastic glass in the bin. I pulled out a couple of tissues from my pocket, walked back to the table and wiped it dry and clean. I hated people who left food court tables sticky and littered with food crumbs.

As I walked out of the mall, my phone vibrated.

It was Derek.

Have you heard what happened?

I smiled, and replied,

No, but I know.

A minute passed. Derek was typing.

I don't know what to say. I owe you BIG!

I stopped at the pedestrian crossing and entered.

Go forth and worry no more, Mr. Francis. My pleasure to be of assistance.

As I walked across the street, my phone buzzed again,

Let's catch up soon. I want to know everything.

I frowned. I cautioned,

Best not. Haven't you heard of plausible deniability? Let's close this chapter forever.

Once I saw the two blue ticks, I deleted everything. Derek saw what I had done and followed suit.

Within a few seconds, the conversation was unrecorded history.

I walked back to our condo, feeling a combined sense of satisfaction and anticipation.

I needed my notebook.

Ishmael's notebook

__ December:

Task 3:
~~James Hong – To neutralise.~~
Location?
Method?
Resources?
DONE.

Task 4:
~~Rahul Sinha – To terminate.~~
Confirm irrevocability
~~Decide approach~~
~~Where and how?~~
~~Resources?~~
DONE.

New Tasks:
MADAM SOON / SOON BOON TAY – TO PUNISH.
JULIA BINTI SHAFIQ – TO COOPT.

EPILOGUE

*O*ur *Sunday night dinner was a success.*
The beer was cold, and the wine was dry. The food was to die for.

For dessert, Nysa had made Thai Red Ruby, a fascinating dish of crunchy water chestnuts coated in bright red tapioca jelly, swimming in a soup of freshly squeezed coconut milk flavoured with pandan leaves. Light, bright and cheerful, it was the perfect cap to an amazing day. We sat in the living room, having seconds and thirds without any thought of our waistlines.

Marianna and Nysa were in buoyant spirits. The expedition to Prime Auto had gone well. Nysa had returned and told me that they had placed a deposit on a deep blue Porsche Taycan, and that it would be delivered on Shahed's birthday.

Of course, the car was to be kept a secret. Just like Marianna's promotion. Why don't these women realise that secrets are dangerous? That they are like dormant volcanoes that can erupt at any time, and cause unimagined destruction?

Also, if Shahed had an ounce of awareness, he should know by now, seeing Marianna's and Nysa's suppressed excitement and sly smiles, that there was something not quite kosher in the state of Denmark. Yes, I know that I mutilate my metaphors.

It was almost 10:30 pm and the children were preparing to leave. Nysa arose and went to the kitchen to pack some of the leftover food for them. Marianna picked up the glasses from the living room and followed her.

I looked at Shahed and smiled. He had seemed a little quieter than normal.

"All well, Shahed?" I asked, generally.

He looked at me. His eyes held something I could not discern.

"Yes, Dad, all well," he said. Then he hesitated, as his eyes slid away.

I waited.

"So, what have you been doing with yourself?" he finally asked.

"Oh, this and that, a couple of small consulting assignments," I said.

He sat up straight. He looked at me again. He took a breath.

"Dad, don't you find it strange that both Greg and James died in such curious circumstances?" he asked.

I looked at him. I was just going to speak, when Marianna returned to the living room carrying a cool bag filled to bursting.

"We have to leave, Shahed," she said, "I have an early start tomorrow."

He broke off his gaze from me. He rose and went to take the bag from her. I got up along with him.

Nysa came in and we spent the next couple of minutes bidding our goodbyes. We waved good night at the elevator.

Nysa preceded me into the apartment.

"Let me clear up, and I will join you in the bedroom," she said, her eyes promising much more than sleep.

I went to the balcony and lit a cigarette.

So Shahed knew. Or suspected.

I looked at the remorseless flow of traffic far below.

Would Shahed be an asset, or would he become a liability? The smoke obscured my vision.

AFTERWORD – TERMINATING AN EMPLOYEE

I hope you have enjoyed the gradual evolution of Ishmael Dollah from CEO to Assassin.

I also hope you are clear about the basic principles of successful termination.

While we may like to believe it to stroke our own egos, most of what we do in the corporate world is not rocket science.

We start with defining our goal – what is it that we want to achieve.

Then, we seek and find information so that we may understand the ecosystem and its components, its drivers, its idiosyncrasies. So that we may be clear about where the root cause, in the person or in the practice.

Once we have identified that the person is a mismatch with the system, and needs to be terminated, we plan and decide our approach.

Once the approach is clear, we plan the resources this

approach needs – information, expertise, tools, processes, people, infrastructure.

Now we have our goal, our framework, our approach and our resources.

It is time to prepare.

We prepare, then we continue to prepare, and finally prepare some more. Once we have completed this, we prepare again. We review our preparations.

Then, we prepare to act. While we are doing so, we remember Churchill's exhortation, "Plans are of little importance, but planning is essential." Even if the scenarios envisaged may never occur, our planning prepares us for situations that we did not plan for.

If everything goes according to plan, great. If it doesn't, we are not stymied. We take the first opportunity that comes and execute.

We complete the termination as humanely as possible.

Confidentiality is key. A termination that is known and talked about can have a domino effect hurting organizational morale. A termination that is quiet and unseen can have a huge positive impact on morale.

Then, we review our preparations, our execution, our post-execution actions.

When the ecosystem stabilises in its new configuration, we are done. The termination is complete and has achieved its objective.

Sometimes, very rarely, the termination may not have proved necessary. Other approaches may have also worked.

That's okay. That's life.

Don't waste your time on regrets. Move on.

AUTHOR'S NOTE

I had fun writing this book.
Whether you enjoyed reading it is another matter.

I am going to continue writing regardless. Did any aspect of Ishmael's character make you feel that he cared about your feelings?

Just wanted to inform you that "Assassins Are Our Greatest Assets" is the second instalment of a pentalogy. It started off as a trilogy, but there are so many people to kill that it is expanding organically.

I hope you read the first book, "Sixty Is The New Assassin"? It is an international bestseller. Don't look like a dweeb in front of your friends and colleagues, buy it now.

The next instalments will be released in 2026 and 2027 -
"There is an I in Assassin" (*A novel guide to managing teams*)
"Assassins Change Plans, Not The Goal" (*A novel guide to agile management*)
"Assassins Don't Preach, They Perform" (*A novel guide to achieving success*)

Each of these books will deliver valuable insights into

the arcane science of management.

In the process, you will also be thrilled, titillated, tensed, and teased by the ongoing saga of Ishmael Dollah, CEO turned Assassin.

Which other management self-help series can promise you this unique combination of boring and fun?

Take care, be good.

Keep your head down.

Stay alive.

THE END

www.ingramcontent.com/pod-product-compliance
Lightning Source LLC
LaVergne TN
LVHW041454170726
843492LV00005B/1228